Echoes of Love

ROSIE RUSHTON

Piccadilly Press • London

First published in Great Britain in 2010
by Piccadilly Press Ltd,
5 Castle Road, London NW1 8PR
www.piccadillypress.co.uk

Text copyright © Rosie Rushton, 2010

A catalogue record for this book is available
from the British Library

ISBN: 978 1 84812 054 9 (paperback)

1 3 5 7 9 10 8 6 4 2

Printed and bound in Great Britain by CPI Bookmarque
Cover illustration by Susan Hellard
Cover design by Simon Davis

PART ONE

✂ CHAPTER 1 ✂

*'One does not love a place the less
for having suffered in it . . .'*
(Jane Austen, *Persuasion*)

ANNA STARED AT THE NEWSPAPER HEADLINE, HER SHAKING hands making the type wobble in front of her eyes. This was all she needed – why today of all days, on top of everything else?

She glanced down the hall towards the half-open sitting room door. She couldn't let her father see this, at least not right now. She knew exactly what effect the photograph and article beneath it would have on her volatile parent; and considering the mood he had been in all morning, there was no way she was going to give him anything else to sound off about.

She scanned the headline, the full force of the wording making her even more certain that she had to keep it from her father. If she hadn't taken a break from practising for her Grade 8 saxophone exam and come into the kitchen to get a drink, she might never have spotted it until it was too late. She couldn't just bin the paper – he would be sure to scour the house till he found it. Under normal circumstances, he'd have read it from cover to cover by now but the early arrival of Marina Russell, Anna's godmother, and the ensuing argument that was still raging between them in the sitting room, had put paid to any kind of normal Saturday morning routine and the paper had been left on the kitchen table untouched.

'Hi – we're back!' The front door slammed and Anna, torn between the overwhelming urge to throttle her two sisters and the determination to keep this latest development from her father, ripped out the offending page and stuffed it into the back pocket of her jeans. She tossed the paper to one side, just as her sisters, weighed down with a variety of brightly coloured, and very expensive-looking shopping bags, burst into the kitchen.

'Where the hell have you been?' Anna shouted, all the tension and anxiety of the past hour exploding in a stream of words. 'Not that I need to ask. You know what? You two are unbelievable!'

'Calm down!' Gaby, her older sister, protested, pushing past her and heading for the fridge. 'You can't complain – we did ask you to come and you said you wanted to practise your sax.'

'You just don't get it, do you?' Anna stormed, cutting her short. 'This is important, and all you two can do is go shopping. Marina's been here for ages and . . .'

'Well, that's one good reason for us not to be, then,' Mallory, her younger sister by just thirteen months muttered, dumping her bags on the table and kicking off her sandals. 'A morning spent in the company of the Voice of Doom or three hours' retail therapy at Bicester? No contest!'

'That's the last place you should have been,' Anna stressed. 'We don't have the cash any more.'

'For God's sake, Anna, chill out!' Gaby sighed, slamming the fridge door shut and ramming a straw into a carton of blueberry smoothie. 'We didn't need cash. We put it all on my card. Dad said he'd clear it.'

'Oh, and you listened to him, right?' Anna retorted in exasperation. 'What planet are you on? Dad hasn't had any work all year, remember?'

'Yes, but . . .'

'He's had to sell the racehorses, he's got rid of the boat,' Anna went on, 'and Marina says he'll have to —'

'*Marina says, Marina says*,' chanted Mallory, pulling a sparkly vest top from one of the bags and fingering it lovingly. 'It's none of her business. No way is she going to spoil my weekend!'

'Anyway, what's the problem?' Gaby asked, running her fingers through her long dark hair. 'Selling all that stuff must have fetched thousands – I guess that's why Dad said we should get ourselves a load of new gear while we had the chance.'

She cast a somewhat disparaging glance at Anna. 'Look, I can hardly turn up at modelling agencies looking like last year's has-been, can I?' she added. As well as studying fashion design in London, Gaby had done a couple of low-key modelling assignments for a freebie newspaper and now had aspirations to become star of the catwalks as soon as possible. She glanced at Anna's faded jeans and downtrodden pumps. 'At least Dad understands how important it is to look good, even if you don't.'

{ 5 }

'It might be more to the point,' Anna muttered, 'if he realised how important it was to stay solvent.'

To her dismay she felt her eyes pricking with unshed tears as she wrenched open a drawer. 'See this lot?' she shouted, throwing a pile of envelopes on to the table. 'Final demands, letters from solicitors and . . .'

'That is absolutely, downright ridiculous!' Anna's words were drowned out by the sound of her father's voice booming from the sitting room. 'Do you honestly expect me to even consider such an outrageous suggestion?'

Anna's stomach lurched. She hated confrontation and she knew full well that the biggest one ever was about to take place.

'Walter, just let me finish.' Even at a distance, Anna could detect a note of impatience under the softer tones of Marina, the woman who had attempted to inject a modicum of common sense into the Eliot household since the death of the girls' mother three years earlier. 'And before I say any more, I really do think that the girls should be in on this.'

'There's nothing for them to be "in" on,' she heard her father stress. 'I've said my piece.'

'Well, I disagree. Girls!' The sitting room door flew open and seconds later Marina, ignoring his protests, came striding into the kitchen. She was a tall, imposing woman, with silver-grey hair swept up in a chignon. Her obvious affection for the Eliot family had caused close friends to speculate that she might marry the widowed Walter. This was never going to happen, partly because Marina was firmly of the view that men were all very useful in their place but that one wouldn't want one under one's feet all the time; and partly because she was far too sensible to tie herself to a man who was not only a spendthrift, but too devoted to his own needs to have much time left for anyone else. She was, however, a frequent visitor to Hampton House, and even had her own ensuite bedroom on the second floor – a leftover from when she had helped nurse their mother; and, as Walter was prone to grumble on a regular basis, she treated the place – and the girls – as her own.

'Ah, you're back – at last!' she commented, eyeballing Gaby, who turned away with a barely disguised look of contempt.

'Now look,' Marina went on, taking a deep breath and perching on a stool, 'we need to chat. Your father and I have had a long talk about the sale of this house and . . .'

Gaby exploded. 'No way would Dad sell this house, now or ever! He promised.'

'Gabriella, your father is in the habit of making promises he can't keep – that's half the trouble,' Marina replied acerbically. 'There's no getting away from the fact that he is deeply in debt and something has to be done. If Walter does what I suggest —'

'He can do whatever he likes – it's none of your business!' Gaby snapped, her face reddening.

'Gaby, of course it's her business,' Anna burst out. 'You know Mummy asked her to look out for us, and anyway, she's only trying to help. God knows, we need all the help we can get.'

'Whatever,' Gaby muttered, picking up the newspaper to immerse herself in the horoscope page. 'Hey, what's happened to the paper? It's a total mess.'

'Now, as I was about to say,' Marina continued, talking over her and tucking an escaping strand of hair back into place, 'I have managed to come up with a solution which might – just might – suit everyone and mean that Hampton House can remain in the family.'

'So we don't have to move?' Mallory said hopefully.

'Well, it's not quite as straightforward as that,' Marina admitted, avoiding her gaze. 'Anna dear, why don't you make a pot of coffee and then we can all sit down with your father and talk this thing through like adults?'

It occurred to Anna, as her sisters stomped moodily out of the kitchen behind Marina and her dad, that making coffee was the easy part. Expecting adult behaviour from anyone else in her family showed a faith that was as touching as it was naive.

Anna pulled the newspaper cutting from her back pocket, smoothed out the creases and, casting an anxious glance over her left shoulder to ensure that her father was still occupied in the other room, scrutinised the photograph – the photograph of Cassandra Wentworth. Anna couldn't look at her without being reminded of Felix. *If it hadn't been for her*, she thought, *I'd still be with Felix.*

She crumpled the paper and shoved it back into her pocket. What was the point of even thinking about it? It only made her miserable – miserable and angry in equal parts. And not just with Cassandra, but with her dad and Marina; and with herself for the way in which she had allowed them both to manipulate her.

'I know I can never replace your darling mummy,' her

godmother had said repeatedly at the time, 'but she was my dearest friend, and I want to try to do what she would have done had she still been with us. And she would have been saying just what your father and I are saying, believe me.'

And I did believe her, Anna thought, breathing in the aroma of percolating coffee. *I was taken in by all that stuff about how Mum always took Dad's side, bolstered his image no matter what, and I should do the same, and show loyalty . . . Oh yes, Marina had done a great job. Right down to that gentle, but often repeated phrase, 'Just imagine what your mummy would be saying right now.'*

Those words had been enough to make her do just what she was told. But now, she wondered whether in fact her mother really would have meant her to give in so easily. Alice Eliot had been a sensible woman who kept both feet firmly on the ground. She was no quitter, and she had always been the one to calm her husband down when his over-inflated opinion of himself threatened to cause trouble yet again.

'Give it six months and you'll have forgotten all about this,' Marina had told Anna every time she found her sobbing in a corner. 'This is just puppy love – it'll pass.'

But Anna hadn't forgotten and it hadn't passed. There wasn't a single day when she didn't think about those magical few months before she messed everything up and lost the most perfect guy in the world.

'Anna? What's taking you so long?' The sound of her godmother's voice snapped her thoughts back to the current crisis. (Was there ever, she wondered, going to be a time when her family would lead a normal, mundane life?)

She dumped the coffee jug on to a tray, tipped the contents of the biscuit barrel on to a plate, took a deep breath, and prepared for the next major upheaval in the Eliot family saga.

As she slid the tray on to the glass coffee table in the sitting room, it struck Anna that it wouldn't be difficult, even for a total stranger, to form a pretty accurate picture of the Eliot family dynamics from a quick glance round the room that morning.

Her father, immaculate as ever in cream linen trousers and a handmade lilac shirt, was frowning into the ornate mirror suspended above the marble fireplace and pulling fiercely at a stray grey hair. Throughout his colourful and somewhat chequered life, her father had had several passions – racehorses, classic cars, yachts, and yes, Anna's mum – but none was as over-riding as his love of himself. Years earlier, when the girls were younger and he was still one of the country's most popular chat show presenters, he had delighted in scouring the internet for reviews of his shows, and far from dodging the paparazzi when out with his family, he had positively encouraged them. His extravagant lifestyle and willingness to share his views on any subject under the sun made him perfect tabloid fodder; his tendency to lose his temper on live TV boosted the ratings – and just as his deep gravelly voice had brought him plenty of work in voice-overs, so his rugged good looks were in demand notably, for a short while at least, as the Face of Pinnacle – 'the cosmetics range for the man mature enough to care for his skin.' It was, Anna thought now, as she poured the coffee, a pity that he hadn't had the maturity to care for his finances while he had still had a job. Several unfortunate outbursts on air just before his wife's death had cost him his job with the BBC, and the disclosure that he was heard to have said that he considered Pinnacle products to be over-priced rubbish but he'd promote them as long as they paid him mega bucks, meant that a new Face of Pinnacle had long since graced the pages of the upmarket magazines.

He had had hopes of a great comeback with his two shows, *Walt on Wednesday* and *Walt at the Weekend*, on ITV3 and for a while it seemed as if his star might once again be in the ascendant. Such hopes had been abruptly dashed after what the press had delighted in calling 'The Walter-gate affair' – something for which Anna knew deep down he still blamed her. She loved her father dearly, but knew that, as Marina was heard to mutter on more than one occasion, he was a media has-been; the only person who seemed oblivious to this fact was Walter himself.

Not that he was the only member of the family who had an inflated opinion of their own importance. Gabriella, three months short of her twentieth birthday, and home from university for a long weekend, was her father's favourite and always referred to as 'the pretty one'. In fact, she was more than pretty; she was stunningly beautiful and knew it. Tall and willowy with a bosom to die for, long dark hair and eyes the colour of cocoa beans, she was at that moment sprawled on the larger of the two white leather sofas, alternately buffing her nails and flicking through the latest edition of *Vogue*, muttering 'That would look so much better on me' or 'gorgeous' at every fashion advert. Gaby had innate style, bags of confidence, and a total lack of sensitivity to the needs of others.

Mallory, at seventeen the youngest of the three and home from boarding school for the weekend, was 'the fragile one' and the only one of the girls to take after their dead mother, in looks if not in character. She was slender, with azure-blue eyes that filled with tears on demand, ash-blond hair that fought against her straighteners on a daily basis, and pale skin that now, in the middle of summer, was dotted with freckles. But while Alice Eliot had been feisty to the end, never once complaining or asking 'Why me?' as she battled the cancer that was to kill her, Mallory was permanently imagining the worst possible outcome from every scenario and looking to other people to rescue her from any situation that she found even mildly challenging. Despite the fact that she could be hugely irritating on a regular basis, Anna felt very protective towards her; since Gabriella didn't have a maternal bone in her body, it had been Anna who had effectively taken her mother's place and cared for Mallory when she was younger and it was a role that she still felt duty-bound to continue, even though she was well aware that Mallory milked it for all it was worth.

Watching her sister now, perched on the window seat with her bright pink mobile phone clamped to her ear, it was easy to guess that she was engaged in the activity she was best at: twisting other people round her little finger. In this case, it was Charlie Musgrove, her boyfriend; Anna worked that out, firstly from the forced coyness in her sister's voice and then by the sudden switch to a pleading 'but you promised me', when there appeared to be a chance that she wasn't going to get to dictate what they did that evening.

And then there's me, thought Anna, catching sight of her reflection in the ornate mirror over the fireplace as she passed her godmother a mug of coffee and a chocolate ginger biscuit. Oval face, dimpled chin, deep-set grey-green eyes and hair the colour of wet straw that was a throwback to her grandmother, from whom she had also inherited her talent for music. Her godmother always referred to her as 'the sensible, clever one' which Anna knew she meant as a compliment but that right now seemed merely a reminder of how boring she was. Her sisters, both of whom she loved dearly, but neither of whom could be called reliable, had more fun than she did; even Mallory didn't lie awake at night worrying about exams, the future, or whether anyone would ever love her again. And neither of them would dream of beating themselves up for every little mistake they made the way she did over the whole wretched Cassandra business. *Stop it*, she told herself. *You messed up. You blew it. Get over it.*

'Right, so now we've all got our coffee,' Marina began, breaking in on Anna's thoughts, 'let me explain what this is all about.'

'If there's any explaining to be done, I'll be the one to do it!' Anna's father turned away from the mirror and strode over to his favourite armchair, brushing an invisible speck from his shirt sleeve, and gesticulating to Mallory to finish her phone call. 'The fact is that, through absolutely no fault of my own . . .' He paused briefly as Mallory, pouting sulkily, flung her phone on to the sofa. '. . . no fault of my own whatsoever, I am experiencing a few minor money troubles.'

'I'd love to know what major ones would be like,' Marina muttered, and received a withering look from Walter.

'The banks are being totally unreasonable, treating me as if I were just some ordinary punter; that lot at ITV3 need their heads examined, and of course, this confounded government couldn't manage a two-year-old's birthday party, never mind stabilising my investments.' He sighed, as if he alone were the fall guy for the government's ineptitude. 'But,' he went on, brightening a little, 'I've made some cutbacks, which along with a few new irons I've got in the fire – aha! *There's* the paper.'

His eyes lit up as he seized the paper from the piano stool where Gaby had thrown it once she had deduced what lay in store for Librans. 'What on earth – the front page is in shreds and . . . good grief!'

Walter shook the paper impatiently as Anna pulled her T-shirt down over her hips in the hope of hiding the slight bulge in her back pocket. 'That wretched paper boy – just stuffs the paper through the letter box – look at this!'

'Walter, just leave it – we must get this thing sorted and time's running out,' Marina said impatiently, glancing anxiously at her watch.

'In a minute, in a minute,' he said, waving a hand at her. 'I had a tip off that I'd be mentioned in the Roving Eye column today.' He began flicking eagerly through to the sports pages. 'Right now, let's see what they've got to say,' he cried. 'The meeting at Goodwood yesterday . . . first race won by Triumphant Too . . . yeah, yeah, blah, blah! Ah, here we are!'

He stabbed the paper with his finger, folded it in half and began reading.

'Listen to this. *Sorely missed in the owners' enclosure was the ebullient presence of Walter Eliot, whose lively wit and generous spirit has been a hallmark of the June meeting for many years.*'

He glanced up from the paper. 'Lively wit – I like that.'

Anna sighed. She loved her father but his thirst for compliments could be very tiresome.

'*Following the sale at the end of last season of his two promising fillies, Go Girl Go and Hampton Heroine,*' he went on, running his finger down the column, '*it is rumoured that Eliott is yet another victim of the economic downturn and concern was being expressed by sources close to the family that since his somewhat public fall from grace . . .* Fall from grace? How dare they!' he spluttered. 'I was the victim of a hate campaign – and what's this?' He stubbed the paper with his finger. '*. . . he may be forced to withdraw his sponsorship of the Hampton House Stakes held every September at this course . . .*'

'Sources close to the family?' he exploded. 'What idiot has been spreading such malicious gossip?' He glared at Marina as if half suspecting her of running off to the press. 'As if I would dream of pulling out of such a high profile commitment. I've sponsored it for years, I have a box there – I mean, what would my friends think if I were to back out now?'

'If they had any sense, which I sometimes doubt,' Marina replied dryly, 'they would consider it the only possible thing to do in the circumstances. Walter, you are broke: for whatever reason, you have no job. You made a pile of money and spent treble. You've been living on credit and goodwill for years, and now both have run out. Accept it.'

She glanced at Walter whose cheeks were suddenly suffused with colour and who looked as if he might have a stroke at any second. 'But of course,' she went on hastily, fearing for Walter's already high blood pressure, 'if you do as I suggest, then within a few years, who knows? You could be living back here again, and racing and . . .'

'What do you mean, living here again?' Gaby burst out, tossing her magazine aside and glaring at Marina. 'You said we didn't have to move.'

'I said no such thing,' Marina reminded her. 'I said this house might not be sold.' She turned to Walter. 'Shall I tell them or will you?'

Since Walter, eyes bulging alarmingly, made no reply other than a muttered expletive under his breath, she went on.

'My suggestion is that your father leases this place out. Selling the horses and cars has helped a bit, but nothing like enough. The current situation calls for drastic measures. The rent for a long-term lease would be quite substantial and what with the stables, and the tennis court, not to mention the planning permission for the barn conversion, which the tenants could invoke, well it's very desirable.'

'But . . .' Mallory and Gaby began together.

'Let me finish. Your father would still own the freehold, the upkeep would be taken care of by the tenants and . . . oh, it's complicated, but the solicitor says that provided you tighten your belts, all of you, and . . .'

'And where would we live exactly?' Gaby asked sarcastically. 'Or haven't you thought of that?'

'Of course I have, and it's a splendid solution,' Marina replied equably.

Anna held her breath; she had a pretty good idea what was coming. Marina had hinted to Anna that she would be delighted with her plan, which could mean only one thing: Marina was going to let them live at Magpie Cottage. It made perfect sense; Marina always said she preferred her London flat, and the cottage (which despite its name was really quite a sizeable house) was only a couple of miles from Kellynch, the Buckinghamshire village eight miles from Fleckford where the Eliots had lived for years; and that meant they would still be within easy reach of all their friends.

'A really amazing opportunity,' Marina went on, with just a hint of nervousness in her voice. 'I have some friends who own a second home, a rather lovely apartment. They're going to Australia for three or four years to help their son set up a business and won't be able to use it.'

Anna's heart lurched. 'An apartment?' she stammered.

'That's right,' Marina went on. 'They're offering it to your father, rent free, because they want someone to keep an eye on it. And because I made it a condition of my fairly sizeable investment in their son's little venture,' she added casually.

'What? Be some sort of unpaid housekeepers? You have to be kidding!' Gaby sneered.

'Precisely,' Walter grunted.

'Hang on a minute,' Mallory interrupted, perking up slightly. 'Where is this apartment? Spain? Italy?'

'Eastbourne,' Marina replied.

Anna felt as if someone had punched her in the stomach.

'Eastbourne?' Mallory cried. 'Are you completely mad? You expect us to live in some grotty seaside town full of geriatrics? No way!'

For once, Anna was in total agreement with her sister. 'We can't move to Eastbourne!' she began. 'What about the band? We've got loads of gigs.'

Anna played tenor saxophone with Wild Chicks, an all-girl jazz quartet made up of her mates from school. They were making quite a name for themselves in the area and she couldn't let her friends down at this late stage.

'And there's my holiday job,' Anna went on.

'Now you're both being silly,' Marina asserted. 'Anna, holiday jobs will be ten a penny in a seaside town and besides, you're leaving school next week; the band will be a thing of the past.'

'No way – we're keeping it going. We'll meet up in the holidays and —'

'And Mallory dear, Eastbourne is really a very stylish place to live these days,' Marina went on, ignoring Anna completely. 'There's the theatre, and concerts, excellent shops, wonderful walking on the Downs and the cliffs and to top it all —'

'But an apartment?' Walter blustered.

'It's not just any apartment; it's a huge penthouse and, even better, it's at Sovereign Harbour overlooking the marina.'

'The marina, eh?' For a moment Walter perked up visibly.

Marina seized her chance. 'I believe some of your sailing friends have boats moored there?' she murmured, moving towards him. 'The Dalrymples?'

Walter inclined his head and gave a faint nod.

'True,' he replied. 'They've just bought a new seventy-five-footer. I suppose they would be delighted to have me on hand to crew for them. Couldn't do them any harm, with my know-how and I'd have no trouble getting into the Sailing Club, not being who I am.'

He rocked back and forth on his heels, the epitome of pomposity. 'And I do believe the Hendersons were talking about keeping their motor cruiser down there,' he went on. 'Not that they have a clue about boats.'

'I don't care if Ellen flipping MacArthur has a whole bloody fleet there,' Gaby muttered. 'What about my social life, my friends?'

'You'll be at college most of the time,' Marina reminded her. 'And there are trains to London every half-hour and you have your car, though you're going to have to pay the running costs yourself from now on – no more money from your father. Maybe you should get a job.'

'And what about me?' Mallory piped up. 'It's OK for those two, but no way am I going to move away from Charlie – not now he's finally asked me out.'

She looked smugly at her sisters. Gaby was between boyfriends (Gaby was frequently between boyfriends on account of no one quite matching up to her exacting standards) and Anna hadn't had a boyfriend since the big bust up. Mallory never missed an opportunity to remind them that, although she was the youngest, she was the one with a serious love life.

'You're away at school all term,' Marina reasoned. 'Obviously you can't leave school in the middle of your A-levels, so that's an expense that'll have to be covered.'

'Look,' Walter burst out. 'I really don't know why you're worrying about all these details right now. There's no need – after all, even if I were to agree to rent this place out, and I'm not saying I will – it will take months to find a suitable tenant and by then . . .'

'I've already found one.'

There was a stunned silence as four pairs of eyes fixed on Marina.

'Quite by chance, and clearly meant to be,' she went on triumphantly. 'You remember my friend Jaspar Shepherd?'

'Which one's he?' Gaby asked somewhat sarcastically. 'I get confused with all your hangers-on.'

Marina had a number of men friends who escorted her to the theatre and to parties ever since Gerald, the one man she had begun to consider as a possible long-term partner, gave up waiting and took himself off to South Africa with a woman young enough to be his grand-daughter.

'The Scottish one,' Marina replied briskly. 'Anyway, he was telling me about these friends of his who have been working all over the world for years and are now back in the UK, and desperate to settle in this part of the world. Childhood memories, apparently.'

'I am not selling,' Walter stressed.

'They don't want to buy,' Marina went on. 'Something about their capital being tied up in overseas funds. Anyway, they want to rent somewhere large enough to have house parties and entertain in style and then decide where to settle in a few years' time when their investments mature. I told Jaspar to get in touch with them right away about this place. He did – and you know what?' She glanced at her watch. 'They'll be here any minute now to take a look!'

For a moment no one moved. They all just stared at Marina, who, after a second, did have the good grace to look just slightly embarrassed.

'You may think I've been a bit presumptuous,' she began, making a show of tidying the pile of glossy magazines on the coffee table.

'And the rest,' Gaby muttered.

'You always were a control freak,' Walter retorted. 'Meddling in things that don't concern you. If it wasn't for the fact that you were darling Alice's best friend . . .'

He turned away for a second to compose himself. Pompous and self-opinionated he might be, but no one could deny his love for his dead wife. His spending had escalated every month since she'd died as if he were trying to blot out his grief the only way he knew how.

'And anyway, who are these people? Do we know anything about them?' he demanded, seconds later. 'I'm not having just anyone living here. I have an image to sustain, a reputation.'

'Exactly,' Marina smiled. 'Which is why I think the Crofts would be perfect tenants.'

It was all Anna could do to suppress her sharp intake of breath at the sound of that name. Surely, it couldn't be? No, it was ridiculous; there were probably loads of Crofts around.

'Croft? Not the sherry people we met at the Harrisons?' For a moment, Walter brightened visibly.

'No, Ruth's an artist and Joseph's an anthropologist. Clever man – goes all over the world recording the oral traditions of threatened tribes or something. Written a couple of books and he's planning a documentary – very well respected.'

It is *them*, Anna thought. *That description couldn't fit anyone else.* She was coming here. Ruth Croft – Felix's aunt. She stared at Marina, astonished that she hadn't made the connection. But then, on second thoughts, why should she? All she and Anna's father had been interested in was splitting Anna up from Felix Wentworth, not analysing his family tree.

Her musings were interrupted by her father's cry of astonishment and the sound of car wheels scrunching on the gravel.

'That's an Aston Martin!' Walter exclaimed, striding across to the window and peering out. 'Are these the people who want this place? Good taste in cars, I'll grant them that – good heavens! They're black.'

'Your point being?' Marina asked sternly.

'Well, I – nothing, I mean, it's not as if I have any prejudices at all, despite what some elements of the gutter press may have cooked up and —'

'So this would be a great opportunity to prove that to the world, wouldn't it?' Marina concluded decisively. 'Now, girls, do go upstairs and check that your bedrooms are tidy – we want to make a good impression.'

I can't do this, Anna thought, as her sisters, muttering under their breath, ambled out of the room. *What if Ruth realises who I am? Felix must have talked to her about me – he told her everything. What if he sent her a photo? He was always emailing pictures to his mates.*

The doorbell chimed.

'Anna, darling, get that will you, while I clear away these cups,' Marina called. 'Quick, quick, we don't want to keep the Crofts waiting.'

Anna's heart was pounding as she walked towards the door.

'And Walter, you will at least consider them as tenants, won't you?' she heard Marina plead above the clatter of crockery.

'I suppose,' her father acknowledged. 'Provided, of course, they seem to be the right type of people moving in the right circles. No skeletons in the cupboard, bad connections, that sort of thing.'

Listening to him going on, Anna knew she couldn't do it. Whatever Marina said, there couldn't be many people in the middle of a recession who could afford the rental on a six-bedroomed house with two acres of garden. If by any chance Ruth Croft did make the connection and mention Felix – or worse still his mother – then no way would her father even consider having them in his house. Her sisters might have their heads buried in the sand, but Anna knew how desperate things were – and how quickly they needed to be sorted.

She turned and ran up the two flights of stairs to her bedroom, as the doorbell rang urgently for the second time. Ignoring the shouts from her godmother, she grabbed the photograph that she kept Blu-tacked to the side of her wardrobe. Standing on tiptoe, she pulled a box from the top shelf, flopped down on the bed and opened the lid, as Marina's cut-glass tones wafted up the stairs as she greeted the Crofts.

For a moment, Anna gazed at the photo, now curling slightly at the edges, and ran her finger gently over Felix's smiling face. Her hand went to the bottom of the box where her journal lay. She resisted the urge to pull it out –

what was the point? Re-reading it only made her miserable, acutely aware yet again of what she'd lost.

She tossed the photograph into the box, shoved it back into the wardrobe and headed for the bedroom door, intent on getting out of the house before she had to face Felix's aunt.

But it was too late. She heard Marina's voice on the stairs.

'And just up this second flight of stairs is another bedroom with en suite shower.'

Within seconds there was a brisk tap on her door.

'Can we come in, dear?'

Without waiting for an answer, Marina opened the door and there she was. Felix's Auntie Roo, easily recognisable from the photos Felix had shown her, and wearing a voluminous yellow and black kaftan with a matching bandana on her head and vast quantities of bangles on her chubby wrists. Behind her, rimless spectacles perched on the end of his nose, was her husband Joseph, a man with graying curly black hair, as slender as his wife was voluptuous, who was already stretching his hand out to shake Anna's.

'This is my god-daughter, Anna,' Marina began. 'She's just finished school and —'

'Oh, but what a lovely room!' Ruth exclaimed, clapping her hands in delight and walking across to the gabled window. 'Just look at that view! Now this will be perfect for when my nephew comes to stay.'

Anna's heartbeat accelerated to such an extent that she felt sure everyone in the room would hear it.

'A bit girly, of course, but nothing a slap of paint and new curtains . . .' She gasped and turned to Anna. 'How tactless of me – you leaving and me already thinking about changing things! What I meant . . .'

'It's fine, honestly,' Anna said, turning away to fiddle with an ornament on her bookcase and fighting against the idea of Felix lying in her bed.

'Hold your horses, precious,' Joseph murmured, glancing fondly at his wife. 'We don't know for sure that he'll come. After all, his mother will want to see him when he gets back.'

'But Joe, Felix has spent part of every summer holiday with us since for ever.'

'That,' Joseph replied gently, 'was when he was a kid. He's a grown man, a soldier . . .'

'And all the more in need of a relaxing break,' Ruth said dismissively, turning to Marina. 'He's a lovely lad, my nephew. My brother's boy, you know. I love him to bits, and not having been able to have children of my own, he's been like a son to me.' She sighed. 'Of course, what with us having been abroad for so long, I haven't seen nearly as much of him as I would like, but we keep in touch with phone calls and email when we can – or rather we did until Joe here dragged me off to darkest Patagonia!'

The affectionate way she smiled at her husband made it obvious that she was more than willing to be dragged anywhere he chose.

'So I haven't seen the dear boy in over a year and now . . .'

Listening to her barely pausing for breath, Anna remembered how Felix used to talk about his aunt's verbal diarrohea.

'He's with the Marines in Afghanistan, you know – such a worry, every time I hear about some poor guy getting killed, I feel physically sick until I know it's not him.'

Anna knew the feeling only too well.

'But a few more weeks, and he'll be home on leave,' Ruth chattered on. 'Just enough time to move in and get the room ready.'

Anna felt the room begin to spin. Felix was coming home. Coming here. And she would be miles away in Eastbourne. At that moment, she realised that Marina was staring at her with a penetrating look. She smiled in what she hoped was a carefree manner and prayed that her godmother hadn't worked out who the Crofts really were.

'What a relief that will be!' Ruth went on. 'And you dear —' She beamed at Anna.

'Excuse me,' Anna gabbled. 'I've got to go, er, out. Lovely to meet you.'

'Anna?' Marina's tone was sternly disapproving as Anna squeezed past them and out on to the landing.

'Me and my big mouth,' she heard Ruth say apologetically. 'The poor child's upset at leaving and why shouldn't she be? You know, I had the strangest feeling just now that I'd seen her face somewhere before.'

Anna, halfway down the stairs, stopped and held her breath, straining her ears to catch the conversation.

'But then again, I meet so many young people, what with my illustration workshops and then trailing around the place with Joe on his lecture tours. Now then, about the rental?'

Anna exhaled with relief. She'd got away with it. Now all she needed to do was keep well out of the way until the Crofts had gone. And try somehow not to think about Felix in her bedroom, in her shower – in short, not to think about Felix at all.

{ 26 }

❧ CHAPTER 2 ❧

'A few months more, and he perhaps may be walking here.'
(Jane Austen, *Persuasion*)

AT THE BOTTOM OF THE LONG GARDEN, TUCKED IN A CORNER behind the fruit trees, and overlooking the field that led down to the river, stood a cream and blue shepherd's hut. It had been the Eliot girls' playhouse when they were small, and still served as a place they escaped to when the need to sulk, scream or simply be alone came over them.

Anna pushed open the door, its hinges creaking slightly, and stepped inside. A shaft of sunlight lit up the faint layer of dust on the rusting wood burner, and a cobweb brushed across her face as she tossed an old magazine aside and slumped into one of the wicker armchairs. Casting an anxious glance through the window to make sure that no one had seen her, she pulled the newspaper cutting from her pocket.

Controversial campaigner and champion of lost causes: our new columnist, Cassandra Wentworth, MP, ensures a challenging read. Catch her every Saturday from July 1st in our Week Ending section!

Just reading the strap-line made Anna cringe inwardly,

but it was one of the photographs in the mini-collage beneath it that she'd been so anxious to keep from her father.

The photo was a still from that fateful programme in the last series of *Walt at the Weekend*. It showed Walter and Cassandra face to face, each looking as if they could cheerfully murder the other. The caption read, *Still confronting issues head to head – Cassandra Wentworth sniffs out the sleaze in high places in our new series. Don't miss it!*

Anna jumped as the door to the hut flew open and Mallory, tears streaming down her face, burst in.

'How can you just sit down here like nothing's happened?' she sobbed. 'You know what? Dad's only gone and agreed to rent our house to those people —'

'He did? It's agreed? Thank God!' So just possibly, her dad wouldn't have to declare himself bankrupt.

'What do you mean? How could you say that? It's just not fair!' She flung herself down on the chair opposite Anna and wiped her nose on the back of her hand.

'Can't you stop him?' Mallory looked up pleadingly.

'Even if I could, it wouldn't be the right thing to do,' Anna replied as gently as she could. 'We can't afford to stay here. If the Crofts hadn't taken it, someone else would have.'

'Mummy would never have let this happen,' Mallory sniffed. 'Us going broke, I mean.'

'I know,' Anna sighed. 'But she's not here and we just have to make the best of it.'

'I'm scared,' Mallory whispered. 'I won't know anyone in Eastbourne and Charlie . . .'

She choked back a sob. 'If I'm not around, he might find someone else and I really love him.'

Anna got up and put an arm round her sister. 'Don't be silly,' she said. 'Anyway, if he was the type of guy to dump you just because you moved house, he wouldn't be worth having in the first place. If you're really right for one another, this won't change it.'

'You don't know anything,' Mallory retorted. 'You haven't been out with anyone since Felix – and that was ages ago.'

Anna bit her lip.

'Do you still miss him?' Mallory asked with rare sensitivity.

Slowly Anna nodded. What was the point of pretending? 'Yes. Every day. I guess I should never have listened to what anyone else said – letting them persuade me to finish with him, it was stupid.'

'You're right!' Mallory leaped to her feet. 'And I'm not going to mess up my life because of what other people do. Dad wants to move, fine. But he's not dragging me with him.' She pulled her mobile phone from the back pocket of her jeans and punched in a number.

'What are you doing?' Anna asked. She knew full well that, however big a tantrum her sister threw, nothing would change.

'Calling Charlie,' Mallory replied. 'Come on, come on, pick up.' She tapped her foot impatiently.

'Hang on a minute,' Anna began, glancing out of the hut window. 'He's coming here.'

'Where are you, for God's sake?' Mallory shouted at the unanswered phone.

The door of the hut swung open again and Charlie Musgrove, grinning from ear to ear, held up his shrilling mobile.

'Hiya babe – how's that for instant response?'

'Charlie!'

In a moment, Mallory switched from impatience to pathos. She flung herself into Charlie's arms and began sobbing with an intensity that, had she been on the West End stage, might have been considered over-acting.

'Charlie, the most terrible thing . . . and I can't bear it . . . and no one understands except you . . . can't cope . . .'

'Hey, hang on – what's happened?' He cast an anxious eye in Anna's direction and raised one eyebrow questioningly.

Charlie, who at nineteen looked two years younger and had the cheeky grin of a small boy caught stealing cookies, was totally besotted with Mallory and either didn't realise, or didn't care, that making a drama out of a crisis was her preferred way of operating.

'My entire life is in ruins,' she sobbed. 'As if I haven't been through enough already what with Mummy and . . . I'll never forgive my dad.'

Charlie patted Mallory's shoulder and looked pleadingly at Anna.

'I'll leave you two alone,' she said briskly and then paused. 'By the way, how is your mum, Charlie?'

Bea Musgrove was recovering from a badly broken arm, the result of getting overenthusiastic at the church Barn Dance.

'In a tizz,' Charlie replied. 'The girl who runs the tearoom has handed in her notice, and Ellie who helps out with the cottages has got glandular fever. And at the height of the letting season too. And what with Mum being one-armed and dad tied up with the harvesting and the farm rides, life's a bit difficult at our place. To say the least!'

'*Your* life's difficult?' Mallory gulped, squeezing a few more tears out of her eyes. 'At least you've got a home.'

'Mallory, don't be so dramatic,' Anna began.

'I thought you were leaving,' her sister snapped. 'So just go – hey wait a sec! You've dropped something.'

She stepped forward and picked up the newspaper cutting from the floor. As she handed it to Anna, her gaze fell on the photograph.

'Hang on, isn't that Cassandra Wentworth?'

'Thanks, I'll take that!' Anna snatched it from her sister's hand. 'Didn't you have something you wanted to tell Charlie?'

'Yeah, babes, I haven't got much time,' Charlie said. 'I only popped in on my way to pick up stuff from the printers for Dad.'

Not surprisingly, Mallory's tears conveniently began flowing again, and the last words Anna heard as she hurried back towards the house were, 'Charlie, if you really love me, you've got to do something. And fast.'

Late on the following Friday afternoon, Anna was sitting in Caffé Nero stirring her latte disconsolately while her best friend, Shannon Smith, demolished a doughnut with the dedication of one warding off imminent starvation.

'. . . and so there's nothing for it, we've got to move to Eastbourne.'

She had been putting off sharing the news for as long as she could in the vain hope of a miracle, but now that Shannon was home from her latest stint in Stoke Mandeville hospital, there was nothing for it but to come clean.

'But you can't!' Shannon spluttered, spraying crumbs over a large area. 'What about the band? We've got all those gigs coming up – you can't just swan off and leave us!'

'I don't want to, but . . .'

'And Felix? I mean, you've been going on for the last heaven knows how long about how much you miss him, and how you wish you could turn the clock back, and now you get a chance to put things right and you're going to chuck it all away!'

'What choice do I have?' Anna asked.

'Anna Eliot, for God's sake get a grip!' Shannon retorted. 'You don't want to go to flipping Eastbourne? So don't go!'

'Oh, like I can really do anything about it? I'm hardly going to rant and rave and throw tantrums like Mallory's been doing, am I? There's enough stress in our house without that.'

'So you're going to wreck your summer, just to keep the peace? And let the band down?'

'You don't understand,' Anna argued. 'On the first of July, the Crofts are moving in – what do you expect me to do? Camp in the garden?'

Shannon sighed, took a long gulp of her coffee, and eyed Anna.

'Right,' she said. 'Question number one: am I your best mate?'

'You know you are,' Anna said, nodding. The two of them had hit it off that very first day in the Sixth Form at Fleckford College, and Shannon was the only one of Anna's friends who knew the whole horrible story from beginning to end.

'Question number two: do best mates tell it like it is?'

'Well, you certainly do,' Anna teased. 'With embellishments.'

'Last question: have you really thought through whether you want to see Felix again? Because it sounds to me as if you're having second thoughts.'

For a moment, Anna said nothing. She'd been wondering the same thing herself for the past week, ever since Ruth Croft had announced that Felix was coming home. On the one hand, if she did see him and he didn't want to know, she might die all over again; on the other, if she didn't see him, and his time away had been filled with yearnings for her and a desire to start over . . .

'A lot. I want to see him a lot.'

'Right,' Shannon said, licking the last remnants of sugar from her fingers. 'So for once, do what you want. You're eighteen, for God's sake – you can do what the hell you like.'

'It's not as simple as that.'

'Oh Anna, those are the very words you said to me way back when everything blew up in your face, remember? And I told you then that things are as simple or as difficult as you choose to make them. Fancy another coffee?'

'I'll get them,' Anna said hastily, as Shannon backed her wheelchair away from the table.

'Don't you dare,' Shannon replied amicably. 'I can manage. Just sit there and make a plan.'

Not for the first time, Anna reflected on the irony of their friendship. There was Shannon, who following a horrendous accident when she was thirteen, spent most of her waking hours in a wheelchair, and who was about the most feisty, go-getty girl she'd ever known, never letting her disability stop her from doing whatever she wanted. She was a great keyboard player, and a leading light of the county wheelchair basketball team. And here was she, Anna Eliot, with everything going for her and the chance to put her whole life back on track, and she didn't have the guts to tell her father that, even if he had to go to Sussex, she didn't have to follow him.

The trouble was, irritating though he was, she loved her dad, and she knew that underneath all his blustering and pomposity, he still missed her mum dreadfully. Alice Eliot had been his rock; his nickname for her had been Pebble, because he said she was too dainty and too beautiful to be a rock. Alice had always been there to pick up the pieces when Walter messed up, always took his side and made excuses for some of his more outrageous behaviour, and one of the last things that she had said to Anna before she died had been, 'Look after everyone, darling. Especially your daddy. You're my sensible girl – I know I can rely on you.'

She'd failed her mum once already. She'd been the cause of all her father's recent problems. She didn't dare upset him again. And yet . . .

Her thoughts were interrupted by her mobile phone vibrating in her pocket.

'Hi Mallory, what's up?'

'You'll never guess, it's so amazing, I could die from happiness.'

'Why? What is it?' Anna laughed.

'I've got a job!'

If Mallory had said that she was about to fly to the moon, Anna couldn't have been more surprised. Work was normally something she expected others to do for her.

'It's so cool,' she babbled. 'I'm going to work in the tearoom at Uppercross Farm. It was my idea and Charlie sorted it with his mum and guess what?'

'What?'

'They say I can live with them all summer till I go back to school. I can have the spare bedroom as my own. And they're going to let me try out recipes for the café and everything. Isn't that just the best thing?'

'Yes, I guess,' Anna replied hesitantly, trying to suppress the surge of jealousy. 'But have you asked Dad?'

'Not yet, and I shan't ask him, I shall tell him,' Mallory replied decisively. 'He can't complain; it's his fault we're in this mess. And besides, it'll look good on my CV for when I go to catering college. Anyway, got to go; Charlie's waiting. Laters!'

For a moment, Anna sat open-mouthed, staring at her phone. While she couldn't for one moment imagine her sister sticking at a job day in, day out, and knew that her latest idea of going to catering college had only come from spending a day on the set of *Ready, Steady, Cook!* when Walter was the guest celebrity, she had to admire Mallory for taking matters into her own hands. In the past, she'd always looked to Anna to take care of stuff and now she was the one getting a life.

That did it. If Mallory could do it, so could she. She'd tell her father today. She wasn't going to Eastbourne either. What's more, an idea was forming in her mind that just might make everything easier.

'I'm not going,' she announced as Shannon wheeled up to the table balancing a tray of coffees on her lap. 'I've decided.'

'Halle-blooming-luljah!' Shannon cheered, punching the air and slopping coffee everywhere. 'So what's the plan?'

'I'm going to ask Marina to let me live with her till I go to uni,' she went on, finally verbalising the idea that had been drifting at the back of her mind for the past two days. 'I mean, I'll go and visit Dad and everything, but if I'm up here, we can still do our gigs.'

The Barn Theatre, on the outskirts of Fleckford, which had grown from a tiny amateur effort in a couple of disused cowsheds into a thriving enterprise that was famous across three counties, had a policy of letting student music groups play in the foyer before shows. Wild Chicks had managed to get slots every week in the summer, as well as the chance to help out from time to time at the theatre's music and drama workshops for kids.

'That's great, but of course not half as vital as being in a position to see Felix when he turns up,' Shannon teased. 'I take it you're not planning to mention that part of the plan to the rest of the family.'

'As if,' Anna replied. 'I guess they'll find out soon enough once he's back home – he'll hook up with Charlie and he's bound to say something to Mallory and once she knows, the entire universe will be informed. Until then, I'm just going to do what the hell I like for once.'

'Too right,' Shannon replied. 'There is, however, a teeny flaw in your plan.'

'Which is?'

'Use your brain, Anna! Let's say you and Felix do manage to get back together. You hang out with one another, text, phone, go clubbing . . .'

'Marina would find out, go mental, tell Dad . . .'

'Exactly. Now, I think you were totally wrong to give in to your family over the whole business last time round, but don't go making it harder for yourself – at least not till you and Felix are together again.'

'But what other choice do I have? I've got to live somewhere.'

'When things really get going, you could always come and stay at my place.'

Anna's mouth dropped open and she stared at Shannon.

'With you? But . . .'

'OK, so I know it's not a patch on your place – we could fit our whole house into your dining room – but we've got a spare room and Mum would be over the moon. I told you she's seeing this guy, Clive?'

Anna nodded.

'He's always asking her to go off for weekends and stuff, and she won't leave me, even though I tell her I can cope. But if you were there . . . you'd be doing us both a favour.'

'It would be brilliant but my dad . . .'

'Hear me out,' Shannon interrupted. 'OK, so you ask Marina if you can move in with her, because that'll keep your dad off your back and keep your godmother oblivious – but as soon as Felix is back and dying to see you . . .'

'Yeah, right.'

'Be quiet. As soon as that happens, you say that my mum wants you to spend some time with me because she's going away. Marina falls for that, you two are totally free to snog yourself senseless and everyone's happy. So go on, ring her.'

'What? Your mum? I can't.'

'Not her, silly; I'll sort her out when the time comes. Ring Marina.'

'Now?'

'Yes – that way I know you're not going to back out and change your mind.'

Anna dialled Marina's phone. 'Hi Marina, it's me. Um . . . there's something I wanted to ask you . . . I was wondering, I mean only if it's OK, but . . .'

'Sound decisive!' Shannon hissed. 'You either want this or you don't. Just do it!'

Three minutes later, Anna snapped the phone shut and grinned at Shannon. 'Sorted!'

'Great!' Shannon spun her chair round to face the door and grinned over her shoulder at Anna.

'And I promise to make myself scarce when you bring Felix back to our place!' she giggled.

The smile faded from Anna's face.

'Like that's ever going to happen,' she sighed. 'I know we don't have a future after what happened, but I just want . . .'

'Stop right there!' Shannon ordered. 'Think positive, imagine yourself in his arms, hear him saying he can't live without you.'

Anna burst out laughing. 'You don't change, do you? You really believe you can make things happen just by wanting them enough?'

'Sure do,' Shannon said. 'I managed ten steps yesterday. On my own. Just one stick. Compared with that, seducing Felix Wentworth should be easy.' She eyed Anna with amusement. 'Hey – you've got that faraway look in your eyes,' she laughed. 'Working out your strategy, I hope?'

Anna shook her head. 'No,' she said. 'I was just thinking about the day we met. Have I told you how he . . . ?'

'Loads of times,' Shannon interrupted. 'I reckon I know more about that evening than if I'd been there myself. But, somehow, I get the feeling you're going to tell me anyway.'

❧ CHAPTER 3 ❧

*'A remarkably fine young man with a great deal
of intelligence, spirit and brilliancy.'*
(Jane Austen, *Persuasion*)

THEY HAD MET AT CHARLIE MUSGROVE'S EIGHTEENTH
birthday party sixteen months ago.

Anna had noticed Felix the moment she arrived: for
one thing, he was the only black guy in the crowded
marquee that had been erected on one of the paddocks at
the Musgroves' farm; and for another, he was seriously hot.
With skin the colour of mocha and short curly black hair,
he reminded her of the lifeguard she had been totally
besotted with on holiday in Barbados when she was
fourteen. He was standing slightly apart from everyone
else under one of the patio heaters borrowed from the
village pub in anticipation of the wintry weather, wearing
faded jeans, a T-shirt and that expression of studied
boredom that guys adopt to cover up feelings of
awkwardness. She hung back in the entrance as Gaby and
Mallory dashed ahead of her, air-kissing everyone in sight
and telling them how great they looked (although Anna
knew that the following day, Gaby would be glued to her

mobile, mouthing off about their apparent lack of style to anyone who would listen), and watched him out of the corner of her eye. He looked about as uncomfortable at the prospect of the evening ahead as she was.

She had never been good at the whole party scene; more than two drinks and she felt sick, and she was useless at the kind of frothy small talk that came as second nature to Gaby. There had been a moment when she almost decided not to come; her attempts earlier that day at colouring her hair Burnished Bronze with Kissed Copper highlights (which *Fab!* magazine had assured her was the look for that season) had been an unmitigated disaster; she looked like a cartoon cockerel and she felt self-conscious and awkward. She was only here because Charlie and his sisters were among her closest friends; the families had known one another since childhood and Uppercross, the Musgroves' farm (which made more money from its self-catering cottages, tearoom and 'Farm Experience' rides than it did from the cattle and sheep that roamed the fields) adjoined the Eliot property and was like a second home to Anna. During her mother's long illness, it had been Bea Musgrove who had made half-terms and holidays more bearable, having the girls to stay and boxing Anna's pony to Pony Club camps and gymkhanas. Anna had even been out with Charlie for a short time in the days when that meant holding hands in the cinema and kissing with lips squeezed firmly together. Not that she'd ever done much kissing with lips apart; she was the only one of her set at her old boarding school who had never had boys texting and emailing twenty-four seven and there had always been those who took delight at the start of every new term in asking whether she had managed to pull over the holidays.

And here she was again, at a party without a boy in tow. Gaby was already wrapped around Zac Harville, with whom she had had a somewhat volatile relationship for the past six months. Mallory, arm in arm with her best friend Olivia, was heading across the marquee towards a group of Charlie's old school mates, and would, Anna knew, within seconds have cornered a partner for the evening. Zac's sister, Phoebe, one of Anna's longstanding mates who lived in the neighbouring village of Drayton Magna, was wearing her usual slightly bored expression as Jamie Benwick gazed at her with his brown, puppy-like eyes. Charlie's sixteen-year-old twin sisters, Louisa and Henrietta, home from boarding school for half-term, were hanging out with a group of boys who were trying to outdo one another in an attempt to show off.

Everyone, it seemed, was deep in conversation. Everyone except the black guy. Maybe if she went up to him . . .

'Anna, hi! It's so great you're here!' Louisa Musgrove came rushing up to her as she was still hesitating in the entrance and grabbed her arm. 'It's been ages since we saw you. Hey, what's with the hair?'

'Don't ask,' Anna groaned. 'I'm thinking of suing the makers!'

'So how are you coping? Is it awful?'

'Is what awful?'

'That state school you're at now,' Louisa said. 'Is it full of chavs?'

The Musgrove twins were still at the same rather exclusive boarding school that Anna and Gabriella had once attended, and where Mallory was still a student.

'Don't talk rubbish,' Anna retorted. 'It's brilliant. People are really friendly and the facilities are amazing and, more importantly, I can do music and politics and philosophy and . . .'

She wanted to add that she was overjoyed to be rid of the cliques and the bitchiness and the way everyone tried to outdo everyone else by having the best clothes and the wildest parties, but since the twins were right in the middle of the in-crowd at Swancote Hall, she thought better of it.

'Rather you than me,' Louisa replied. 'I mean, those kind of schools – people go around brandishing knives and stuff. I read in the paper only the other day that . . .'

'Lou, do shut up!' Louisa's twin sister, Henrietta, pushed her way through the clusters of partygoers, a glass of champagne in each hand, and grinned at Anna. 'Honestly, she watches too much *Waterloo Road*!'

She handed Anna a glass and took a sip from her own.

'So come on – are there lots of hot guys there?' Henrietta, dark and petite like her twin, was boy mad, something that being at an all-girls' school did little to appease.

'Not as hot as him,' Anna murmured, glancing towards the tall guy. 'Who is he?'

'Don't know his name,' Henrietta replied, sipping her champagne. 'It's all a bit embarrassing, really. Zac just turned up with him – well, seeing as how Zac is one of Charlie's best mates, we had no choice but to say it was OK for him to stay, did we? Total gatecrasher or what?'

'Shh!' Anna hissed, but she could see from the expression on the guy's face that it was too late. 'He heard you.'

'Serve him right,' Henrietta muttered.

'You'd better go and chat him up and make peace then,' Louisa teased. 'It's pretty obvious you're into him.'

'Don't be so silly.'

'Lulu's right,' Henrietta added. 'You've been eyeing him up the whole time we've been talking.'

'You go,' Anna said. 'You're the one who was mouthing off.'

'No way, he's not my type,' her friend replied. 'Leo Hayter's here – now that is one seriously hot guy!'

Leo was the seventeen-year-old son of the new Rector of Kellynch and already had every teenage girl in the area drooling over his film-star looks, inherited from his Italian mother, and the rumour that, while his father might be pure and holy, he certainly wasn't.

'I think he really fancies me,' Henrietta whispered. And with that, she winked at Anna and drifted off towards the makeshift bar, followed closely by her sister.

Anna was still wondering what to do when she saw the black guy head towards the exit. On impulse she pushed her way through the crowd and stepped in front of him.

'Hi,' she said. 'I'm Anna and . . .'

'And I'm Felix, otherwise known as the gatecrasher,' he replied. 'But . . .' He dumped his empty glass on a nearby table. '. . . since I'm leaving, that's not a problem, is it?'

'You can't go!' Anna exclaimed. 'It's not your fault Zac dragged you along. And knowing him, he probably made out it had all been arranged.'

'He did make it sound like it was a free-for-all,' Felix admitted. 'If I'd known it was going to be a posh affair like this . . .'

'It's hardly posh,' Anna laughed. 'Hog roast, bucking bronco and a disco in the barn – it's pretty low-key really.'

'Depends what you're used to, I guess.' He shrugged. 'Anyway, I'm off. It's clear the family don't want me here.'

'Oh for goodness' sake,' Anna retorted following him. 'Ignore Louisa – she's lovely but she never knows when to stop. Anyway, think about Zac.'

He stopped dead in his tracks and stared at her. 'Zac? Why?'

'It's obvious,' Anna replied. 'You go off, Zac will feel bad about it and come after you – and his evening will be ruined too.'

'I doubt he'd notice,' Felix commented dryly. 'He's far too busy moping over that girl.' He jerked his head in the direction of Gaby. 'The loud one with the boobs hanging out of her dress.'

'My sister,' Anna smiled.

'Oh God, my turn to put foot firmly in mouth.' He cringed and looked at her appealingly. 'She doesn't look like you – is she really your sister?'

'Regrettably, yes. Why?'

'Only that she must be the girl Zac's been going on and on about all day,' he sighed. 'Gaby, isn't it?'

'Mmm.'

'It's been Gaby this and Gaby that and how he's never felt like this about any other girl and he's dreading having to tell her . . .'

He paused, clearly embarrassed.

'Tell her what?' Anna asked.

'Nothing,' Felix replied hastily. 'Knowing him, he'll chicken out anyway.'

He frowned, glancing across at them once again. 'I just – well, somehow I didn't picture her as the glam, fashion babe type. The girls he goes for are usually much less flashy – more like you.'

'You weren't thinking of going into the Diplomatic Service by any chance?' Anna asked. 'Because if you were, forget it.'

Felix pulled a face and laughed. 'No honestly, I meant it as a compliment – look, can we start again? I'll pretend I'm a regular guest, and you can pretend I'm not a total idiot.'

Anna burst out laughing. 'Deal,' she said. 'On one condition.'

'And that is?'

'You get me a drink and we talk about something more interesting than my sister's love life.'

'Sounds good to me,' he said, nodding.

As he pushed his way towards the trestle tables laid out with drinks, Anna was conscious of her sisters eyeing her in amazement. And it hit her that, for the first time in her life, she might just be on her way to pulling a guy. All she had to do now was make sure she didn't blow it.

'So how come you know Zac?' Anna asked later, as, after dancing for ages, they queued at the hog roast.

'He used to live next door to us in Fleckford – that was before his parents divorced and he moved to Kellynch with his mum,' Felix replied. 'Then he won a sports scholarship to that posh school where Charlie goes, but we stayed mates. He's cool, not like . . .'

He broke off, clearly embarrassed at what he had been about to say.

'And that guy over there? Jamie, isn't it?' he went on. 'I've met him a couple of times when I've been staying with Zac. Isn't he the one who got that part in *Emmerdale*?'

'Yes,' Anna laughed. 'If you can call it a part – two episodes and a total of eighteen words! But I guess it's a start. You know he's at RADA?'

'He got there? Nice one!' Felix said. 'Zac teased him like crazy about being a total wannabe!'

Anna smiled. 'So what are you doing? Gap year? Uni? You're not at agricultural college with Charlie, are you? Or are you working?'

She knew she was babbling, but looking into those dark eyes appeared to have an odd effect on both her tongue and her brain.

Felix grinned. 'Would it be quicker if I just handed you my CV?' he teased, passing her a plate and gesturing towards the table loaded with slices of pork, bowls of coleslaw and piles of baked potatoes. 'Food first, life history and career plans later. OK? Besides, if I tell you too much too soon you might lose interest, and I don't want that to happen.'

'You don't? Really?' The second she had said it she realised how totally uncool she was being.

'Course not,' he replied. 'I mean, who the hell else am I going to chat to if you do a runner? Even Zac's ignoring me. You're my last hope.'

'You do know you're making a total idiot of yourself, don't you?'

Anna was in the middle of retouching her make-up in the Portakabin loos a couple of hours later when Gaby burst in, cheeks flushed and a none-too-happy expression on her face.

'What do you mean?' Anna asked. 'Falling off the bucking bronco three times in a row? I know but it was such a laugh and —'

'Not that!' Gaby replied. 'The way you're coming on to that guy all the time. You've hardly spoken to anyone else.'

'That's so not true,' Anna protested, unscrewing her mascara wand. 'We talked to Jamie and Phoebe for ages, and to Hen and Leo – she's really got the hots for him! Felix and me, we're going clubbing with them next Saturday because Leo's got these freebie passes for Clouds.'

'Oh? So it's "Felix and me" now, is it?' Gaby replied sarcastically. 'Well in that case, you can tell him to keep his nose out of Zac's life!'

'Gaby, what are you on about?' Anna asked. Gaby always got confrontational when she'd been drinking vodka.

'You know I'd asked Zac to come on holiday at Easter, right?' Gaby fumed, slamming her make-up bag on to the washstand. 'I'd got it all planned and now he says he can't come.'

'Why?' Anna frowned.

'You won't believe this,' her sister replied. 'I don't suppose this Felix has got round to telling you he's going into the Royal Marines?'

'Yes, he sounded keen.' It had been the one time when his face had lost the slightly anxious, haunted expression that she found both disturbing and endearing. 'Mind you, he's failed once but he sounds determined to make it this time.'

'Yes, well he's only gone and persuaded Zac to apply too.'

Anna frowned. 'Persuaded him? But I thought the

Forces was what Zac had in mind all along,' she reasoned. 'Surely he only put it off this long because of that hiking trip he went on – and then he broke his ankle and couldn't do the fitness test. When we were at Phoebe's party on New Year's Eve, he said he couldn't wait.'

'I know he did say all that but then I reminded him that he'd never get to see me, and told him I was not going to hang around for some guy who was never home and might get himself blown up at any minute.'

'Gaby, you didn't? That's emotional blackmail!'

'So what? It worked. A few weeks back, he told me he loved me so much that he was going to apply to the police instead. Now it seems Felix has got him to change his mind.'

'But what's all that got to do with you and Zac going on holiday?' Anna asked.

Gaby looked close to tears. 'They've got this assessment next week, right?'

Anna nodded.

'And if they get in, Zac says they'll be starting a couple of weeks after Easter and he wants to spend the time preparing, not going to Ayia Napa.'

Anna sighed. 'Well, he might not get in – it's pretty difficult.'

'He says he's not up for it – he can't talk about anything but training and getting fit,' Gaby muttered. 'Anyway, I've told him, it's the Marines or me.'

She pushed open a cubicle door, and paused, turning to Anna. 'And by the way, if you've got any sense, you won't even think about getting involved with Felix. I mean, what do you know about him?'

'Who said anything about getting involved? I only met him three hours ago, for God's sake!'

There was no way she was about to admit to Gaby that she had been praying all evening that he'd ask her out.

'As far as I'm concerned,' she went on as nonchalantly as she could, 'he's just a really nice guy.'

'With some seriously big issues,' Gaby concluded, slamming the cubicle door shut and sliding the bolt. 'Zac says —'

'I don't want to know what Zac says,' Anna interrupted.

'Suit yourself,' her sister replied. 'Don't say I didn't warn you.'

'So how do you feel about us hanging out some place one evening?' Felix said an hour later, dancing closer to Anna than anyone had ever done before and running his hands slowly up and down her back. 'Before next weekend, I mean. Thing is, I really like you, Anna – you're kinda, oh I don't know.'

'Gorgeous? Witty? Totally amazing?' Anna teased, gasping inwardly at her own audacity. Never before had she felt confident enough to chat this easily with anyone, let alone someone she had only known for three hours and whose mere touch was enough to send shivers down her spine.

Felix laughed. 'All that, of course,' he replied. 'But I was going to say you're so normal.'

'Oh. Now on a scale of one to ten, that scores about two and half in the compliment ranking!'

'Trust me, when you've got a family like mine, normal is good.'

'So tell me about them,' Anna said quickly, recalling Gaby's insinuations earlier that evening.

'You really don't want to know,' he said, pulling away slightly and looking her straight in the eye. 'Ever since I got home from my gap year – well, gap six months – we've been . . .' He faltered and then grinned. 'Well, let's just say that right now we're not exactly a role model for happy families.'

'Right,' Anna murmured, not really knowing how to respond.

'But actually, tonight I'm glad I had a bit of a bust up with Mum,' he said, 'because I only turned up at Zac's on the spur of the moment to escape the fallout and now I've met you and . . .'

He didn't say any more. He gently tipped Anna's chin and drew her towards him. The kiss when it came was all she had imagined it would be.

And the astonished expression on Mallory's face as she walked by with Olivia just added to the magic of the moment.

As the DJ put on the last song, Anna was on cloud nine. Not only did she find Felix the easiest person in the world to be with, but she had rather enjoyed the sidelong glances and whispered comments from her mates as they jostled one another on the dance floor.

'Sexy or what?' Phoebe Harville had mouthed, as she and Jamie danced beside her. 'Nice butt!'

'Well, you certainly made him welcome!' Louisa muttered under cover of a particularly noisy rendition of 'Hug Me, Love Me, Snog Me Senseless' from Charlie's old school mates.

{ 51 }

'Got in there fast, didn't you, Felix?' Zac had teased, one eye on his friend and the other on Gaby, who was blatantly flirting with one of his friends on the opposite side of the marquee. 'See – there are things more interesting than ten-mile runs and hours on the treadmill!'

That's when his forced grin wavered and he turned to Anna. 'You two are coming out with us lot next Saturday, right?' he asked.

Anna glanced at Felix and then nodded.

'So – well, see, Gaby – she's upset because – well, the thing is I'm going to try for the Marines, and now she says she doesn't want to know.'

'She'll come,' Anna cut in quickly. 'She's always moody when she's been drinking vodka tonics. She never learns.'

Zac's face brightened so much that Anna felt instantly guilty for giving him false hope.

'Yeah, that'll be it,' he said confidently. 'I'll give it a day or so and call her. You two can drag her along, right? Cool.'

Anna smiled at him, but the smile had more to do with the thought of being with Felix than with any hope that her sister would change her mind.

'Hey, wait!' Felix grabbed Anna's arm at the end of the evening, as she made her way towards Gaby and Mallory who were gesticulating wildly at her. 'I haven't got your phone number.'

He fumbled in his pocket and pulled out his mobile phone. 'Go on, tell me.'

She watched as he punched the numbers into his phone.

'Great!' he said. 'Look, I'll call you, OK?'

'Sure,' Anna said enthusiastically. 'It's half-term this week so I'm free pretty much all the time.'

'The trouble is,' Felix began, and Anna's heart sank, 'Zac and I are doing the Mountain and Moor Challenge from Monday to Thursday. It's going to be pretty full on, running, fly camping, canoeing and all against the clock.'

'Sounds like hard work,' Anna shuddered.

'Good training though, for the fitness test for the Marines next week,' he pointed out. 'But it does mean I won't be around. But I'll call you Thursday evening and sort out something for Friday, yeah?'

'That'd be cool,' Anna said. 'Can't wait.'

'Can't wait for what?' Gaby demanded, as Felix disappeared to find Zac.

'Friday – he asked me out – well, as good as!' Anna couldn't suppress her excitement.

'Oh wow, big deal!' her sister scoffed. 'You do know it's totally desperate to look so enthusiastic with someone you've only just met? If you want my advice . . .'

'I don't,' Anna replied calmly. 'In fact, I can't think of anything I want less.'

❧ CHAPTER 4 ❧

'How quick come the reasons for approving what we like.'
(Jane Austen, *Persuasion*)

FOR THE WHOLE WEEK FOLLOWING CHARLIE'S PARTY, Anna hadn't been able to get Felix out of her mind. Not that she had tried very hard; she went over and over their conversations in her head, recalled his kiss in its minutest detail every night as she fell asleep and even went back to the childish habit of scrawling A ♥ F all over her journal. She knew it was crazy; but never having had a real boyfriend before, she wanted to do all the things her mates did and do them all at once. Just in case.

And at last Thursday evening came.

And he didn't phone.

All evening Anna kept setting herself goals and making excuses for his silence.

'He'll be exhausted and having a shower and then he'll ring.'

'If I practise my saxophone for twenty minutes, he'll ring – no, I might not hear the phone.'

'I'll count to one hundred in Spanish and then he'll . . .'

'Why do you keep looking at your watch?' her father,

who was indulging in a very vocal case of man flu, asked in exasperation at nine-fifteen.

'It's a guy!' Gaby looked up from the Flats To Let section of the *Evening Standard* and raised an eyebrow. 'He said he'd call her and like an idiot, she believed him.'

'What? You mean, Anna's got a boyfriend?' Walter looked as surprised as if Gaby had announced that Anna had installed a baby elephant in the back paddock.

'He's not a boyfriend,' Anna said at once. 'He's just . . .'

'A *really nice guy* . . .' Gaby mimicked. 'Except he's not. He's black and has a real Fleckford accent.'

'Why on earth —?' Walter began.

'And he gatecrashed Charlie's eighteenth,' Gaby concluded with a sneer.

'Now *that*,' Walter declared, 'is simply not done. As anyone would know.' He looked at Anna. 'I knew things would go from bad to worse when you insisted on leaving Swancote Hall.'

'What's more,' Gaby butted in, 'he's trying to break me and Zac up.'

That did it for Anna. 'That's so not true!' she exploded. 'You're the one who's dumping him if he joins the Marines.'

'What? I thought Zac had abandoned that ridiculous idea,' Walter exclaimed.

'Me too,' Gaby sighed.

'Well, in that case, you're being very wise, darling.' Walter nodded approvingly at Gabriella. 'You're young, beautiful and talented – why tie yourself to someone who's about to disappear for months and probably end up dead.'

'Dad! That's an awful thing to say,' Anna protested.

'Face facts.' Her father shrugged. 'Gaby's too good for a run-of-the-mill raw recruit anyway. Now, tell me Gaby darling, what ever happened to that lovely Fanshawe boy?'

Anna was tempted to say that the lovely Fanshawe boy had dumped Gaby months before because he said he couldn't afford her expensive tastes. But she was too busy waiting for the phone to care about anything else.

At eleven o'clock, having checked her mobile and the landline at ten-minute intervals all evening, Anna went to bed. She had been, she thought miserably, just the kind of idiot Gaby thought she was.

Anna was wandering listlessly around the house late on Friday morning, silently berating herself for even caring about someone who had clearly forgotten her already, when the phone rang. Heart pounding, she grabbed it.

'Hi, it's Shannon.'

'Oh. Hi.' Anna's heart plummeted.

'I'm thrilled to hear you too,' Shannon teased. 'What's up?'

'Nothing – did you have a good half-term at your gran's?'

'Don't change the subject,' Shannon ordered.

'It's just that I met someone at a party last Saturday and he said he'd ring, but he hasn't and I thought when you rang it might be him and . . .'

'A boy? I need details. What party? Why wasn't I invited? What's he like?'

'It was these mates of mine from the village and . . . oh my God! Shannon, sorry, I've got to go. My mobile's ringing – it could be him!'

'Go girl!' Shannon laughed. 'Call me back. Soon!'

'OK, bye!' Anna punched the *Answer* button.

'Hello?'

'Anna? Hi, it's Felix. I am really sorry I didn't get back to you last night, but . . .'

'No problem,' she said, trying to sound as if she had only just remembered he was meant to call her. 'How was your week?'

'Great – and then I was on my way back and got this phone call from . . .'

'Hang on, you're breaking up,' Anna said in panic.

' . . . phone call from Ruth . . . love her to bits . . . couldn't bear not to see her . . . so . . . and . . . with her now and . . .'

And then the connection died.

Anna slumped down on a chair. He was with a girl. And he hadn't made any secret of it, which told her everything she needed to know and . . .

The phone rang again.

'Anna, sorry! Lost the signal. Look, in case it goes again – can we meet in about an hour? Is that OK? Something I need to tell you. Anna? Are you there? Anna?'

'What? Me? Meet up with you?' She hesitated. 'The two of us?'

Felix burst out laughing. 'Yes, I think you have all the relevant points there. Well? Is that a yes, a no, or a maybe?'

'Yes, sure – that's great. Where?' She knew her voice sounded flat, but she had a pretty good idea what it was he wanted to tell her. That it was over before it had even started.

'I'll pick you up. I'm in Fleckford and Mum's using her

car, so I'll have to get the bus. Remind me how to get to your place?'

'It's complicated,' Anna replied swiftly, the thought of introducing Felix to her father being a bridge too far right now. 'And I've got a car – so how about we meet in Fleckford? How about The Boatman, down by the river?'

'Cool,' he agreed. 'See you then!'

Fifteen minutes later, when the entire contents of her wardrobe was flung on her bed and on the floor and she was despairing of ever getting her hair to look halfway presentable, Gaby burst into the room.

'I need you to come shopping with me,' she declared. 'I can't go to Sophie's party in anything I've got already. I'm going in ten mins, OK?'

'Sorry, I can't,' Anna replied calmly, stepping into her skirt and tugging at the zip. 'I'm going out.'

'Out? Where? Not with that Felix guy?'

The split second pause before Anna answered was enough for Gaby to suss that she had hit on the truth.

'Have you told Dad?'

'Not yet.'

'Dad! DAD?' Gaby had shot downstairs before Anna could open her mascara. In the event, it occurred to her that eye make-up was less important than a quick escape. She slipped downstairs and out of the back door. It was going to be bad enough getting dumped by Felix, without facing an inquisition from her father.

Anna had always been totally dismissive of chick lit books that talked about the effects a boy could have on an apparently sane female with more than her fair share of brain cells. She'd always assumed that phrases like 'she went weak at the knees' or 'she lost herself in his smouldering gaze' were evidence of a total lack of both perception and command of the English language on the part of the author. Now she wasn't so sure. The smell of him when he hugged her, the firmness of his grip as he held her hand at the bar, and then led her to a table in an alcove by the roaring log fire, the way his nose went all squashy when he grinned – everything about him made her go crazy.

'I just had to see you before we go out with the others tomorrow,' he said. 'I mean, I don't know anything about you really and yet I feel I've known you for ages. So come on, tell me all about you.'

'There's not much to tell,' Anna replied awkwardly, wondering whether he'd been doing the same chat-up line with this Ruth girl hours before. He didn't sound like someone who was about to finish with her; but then again, maybe he was going to tell her that Ruth would be coming along the following day as well.

'Come off it, everybody's got a story,' Felix had urged. 'I mean, I know you've got two sisters, one of whom has just broken my best mate's heart – he hardly talked about anything else all the way up Pen y Fan.'

'She'll probably come round,' Anna assured him. 'She's like that – goes into total meltdown and then spends weeks regretting it.'

She paused for a moment and then sighed. 'I do think she's crazy to give up on someone as nice as him, so let's hope she comes to her senses.'

'And so you'd be OK hanging out with a guy who joined up? Went to war, even?'

Those dark eyes were still penetrating into her very soul. Her heart rate quickened, her mouth went dry as she took a deep breath.

'If I had a boyfriend I really cared about, then what he did wouldn't make any difference,' she replied. 'As long as it was legal!'

'Oh good,' he said. 'I'm very relieved to hear it.' He grinned at her and slipped his hand into hers. Her heart went into overdrive and she turned to gaze through the window at the swans on the river in the hope that he wouldn't see the flush that she knew had flooded her cheeks.

'OK, so come on – if you weren't sitting here with me right now, what would you most like to be doing?'

Anna frowned. It was hard to think of one thing better than being with Felix.

'OK,' she said slowly. 'I guess playing my saxophone with an awesome jazz band – preferably somewhere tropical that had white sand beaches and huge ice creams!'

She spent the next twenty minutes filling him on her passions (jazz, books, horses and tapas) and her loathings (maths, heights, the smell of popcorn and all forms of reality TV).

'That is so weird,' he said. 'I thought I was the only person on the planet who hated reality shows.' He took a sip of his drink. 'And chat shows – I hate those, especially the ones where . . .'

He stopped in mid sentence and pulled a face.

'Oh God, there I go again. I forget your dad's on TV and . . .'

'You know who my dad is?' Anna's heart sank.

Felix nodded. 'Zac told me,' he admitted.

{ 60 }

'And that's why you've asked me out.' She couldn't conceal the note of irritation in her voice. 'Because if it is . . .'

'Don't be silly, of course it's not,' Felix said. 'I've never even seen your father – I've more interesting things to do with my life than sit around watching TV.'

Anna smiled. 'That's a relief. Sorry, I get a bit sensitive about it,' she confessed.

'Why? Because your dad's so, well, direct?' He laughed.

'I thought you didn't watch the show.'

'Zac filled me in – said that he's had a few run-ins in the past, and now he goes just about as far as he can go without getting sacked.'

'He's outspoken, that's for sure,' Anna admitted. 'But what really gets me is the way all my friends at my old school angled to get invited to my place, not because they wanted to be with me, but just so they could meet my dad. And when they did, he ended up being so totally over the top and embarrassing.'

'If you're talking embarrassing parents, I bet my mother could give your dad a run for his money any day! The way she goes on and on . . . Oh. Sorry.'

'What for?'

'Zac mentioned about your mum dying,' he said hesitantly.

'It's OK,' Anna assured him. 'What about your dad?'

'They don't live together any more,' he said shortly. 'Anyway, let's just concentrate on us, right?'

'Us?' If he was thinking of two-timing her with this Ruth girl he had another thing coming.

'Yes.' Felix leaned towards her, cupping her face in his hands.

Part of Anna's brain was insisting that she push him away, insisting that she demanded to know the truth about Ruth. But the kiss that followed made the construction of even the simplest sentence a total impossibility.

They drove into Fleckford to see what was on at the cinema, and Anna couldn't resist glancing in the shop windows, revelling in the reflection of herself holding hands with this tall, muscular guy, beside whom she looked almost petite and dainty. Suddenly, the disastrous hair colour with its unfortunate streaks seemed original and edgy and she marvelled at the way in which she could be herself with Felix, feeling absolutely no need to say anything clever or witty. But the best thing of all was that with him, she felt bubbly and vivacious and more like the other girls her age than she had ever felt before.

There was just that one thing lurking at the back of her mind. It was when they had abandoned all idea of a movie – she hated horror films and he couldn't stand the thought of another vampire movie – and were walking up Chinnor Hill to the Ridgeway, a few flakes of snow falling from a leaden sky, that she could stand it no longer.

'Who's Ruth?' She hadn't meant it to come out quite as abruptly.

'Ruth? She's my aunt – my dad's sister – and she's over from Barbados for a flying visit.'

'Your aunt? I thought . . .' She checked herself quickly.

'You didn't think it was a girl?' he asked, mischievously.

Anna said nothing.

'And if it had been, would you have minded?'

'No, of course not . . . Yes, a bit,' Anna replied, avoiding his gaze.

'I wouldn't have asked you out if I'd been seeing someone else,' he said. 'You're not with anyone, are you?'

Anna shook her head.

'Great.' He eyed her anxiously. 'I guess you think I'm a bit of a saddo, wanting to spend time with a slightly eccentric sixty-three-year-old, when I could have seen you earlier, but she's hardly ever in England and . . .'

'It's OK, you don't have to explain,' Anna interrupted, not caring about the details now she knew who Ruth was.

'I want to,' Felix assured her earnestly. 'See, she's always been there for me. Always treated me like an equal. Does that make any sense?'

'I know what you mean,' Anna nodded. 'Bit like my godmother, I guess; since Mummy died, she's the one person I can really be up front and myself with. No pretence, no worrying about saying the right thing . . .'

'Exactly!' Felix replied, tightening his grip on her hand. 'Roo never goes mental or tells me how to live my life. Which is more than I can say for some people.'

'And your parents do?' Anna ventured, recalling in minute detail the rows she'd had with her father when she announced that she wanted to leave Swancote Hall and study music and politics at Fleckford College and the way Marina had fought her corner.

'My mother certainly does,' he sighed. 'When I told Roo this morning about trying again for the Marines, she was so over the moon about it, really behind me. Whereas my mother . . .' He fell silent and shook his head.

'Maybe your mum's just scared for you,' Anna suggested.

'You know, ending up in the middle of a war zone.'

'I don't think she's scared exactly,' he replied. 'See, she's an out and out pacifist – or at least that's what she calls herself. Exhibitionist more like . . .'

'How do you mean?'

'For years, every protest march going – she'd be on it. Not just the war in Iraq or petitions to Downing Street – oh no! Want someone to tie themselves to a tree or lie down in front of a bulldozer? Ask my mother. Don't get me wrong – in some ways, I guess it's good that she stands up for what she believes in. She has every right to do that – it's just the way she tries to convert everyone else to her way of thinking that gets to me.' He paused for a moment, scanning the view. 'You know what? She used to drag me along on marches with a placard strapped to my buggy when I was too young to know what was happening. I think she only did it to attract the press.'

Underneath the strident anger in his voice, she could detect a note of real hurt.

'Maybe it wasn't that,' he continued. 'I don't know. Maybe I was just in the way.'

'No, I'm sure . . .'

'See, I'm the afterthought, the mistake, the kid that should never have happened. My brother and sister were both teenagers when I came along. By the time I was at primary school, Oscar and Skye were at uni and off her hands. I was a nuisance. An obstacle in the Rise and Rise of Cassandra Wentworth.'

'Cassandra Wentworth? You mean, she's your mother? But she's . . .' She had been about to say 'she's white' and bit her tongue just in time.

'See? Even you've heard of her.' Felix paused and leaned against the trunk of an oak tree. 'So what was it? The time she threw all those knickers out of that department store window because they weren't Fair Trade cotton? Or maybe when she stormed in on *News at Ten*, supporting animal rights protestors?'

'Actually,' Anna admitted, 'I only know about her because of my dad. He wanted her on the programme after the knicker thing but she refused. She said . . .'

'*I am too busy walking the walk to sit around talking the talk,*' Felix mimicked.

'Yes,' Anna laughed. 'Actually, I thought that was a pretty clever line.'

'It's one of her pet phrases,' Felix replied. 'She's using it as her campaign slogan.'

'So what's she campaigning about this time?' Anna asked.

'She's into politics now – wants to be an MP,' he said. 'She's hoping to stand as an Independent candidate at the Muckleborough and Bythorn by-election. Championing the cause of those with no voice – that's her other catchphrase. As if!'

'But that's wonderful,' Anna exclaimed. 'Rooting for the underdog and all that – sorry, don't get me going. I adore politics. I'm doing it for A-level.'

'Really?' Felix stared at her in disbelief.

'Mmm. I'll need it for the future. Hey, just think – if your mum gets elected, she'll get the chance to do some real good.'

'Oh sure,' he replied cynically. 'She's more about saying one thing and living another.'

Anna was beginning to feel uncomfortable. Her own father could be a pain in the neck sometimes, but she couldn't imagine talking to a comparative stranger about him in that kind of way.

'You're lucky to have your mum around,' she said softly.

He put an arm round her shoulder. 'I know, I know, and I'm sorry – I guess I'm just wound up at the moment because of what's happened, but you're right. She's doing her thing, and I'm going to do mine, no matter what she says. Like Roo's always telling me, you only have one go at life.'

He smiled ruefully. 'You're not really serious? About wanting to be a politician?

Anna shook her head and laughed. 'No, not a politican. I want to be a political correspondent. I'll do a degree in politics, and then maybe a Masters, get an internship . . .'

Felix laughed. 'So you've got your life mapped out then?'

'No more than you have,' she said. 'I guess when you want something enough you just have to do whatever it takes to get it.'

'You're right,' he replied. 'See, I knew we had loads in common.'

She glowed under his affectionate gaze. Little did she know that afternoon how her own words would come back to haunt her.

They had been sitting in Anna's car, saying a lengthy and somewhat hands-on farewell, when Felix's mobile rang.

'Hello? Roo – hi!'

Anna made to get out of the car and give him space, but he gestured to her to stay put.

'What's that? Tomorrow evening? Oh. No, sorry. I'm supposed to be going out with some mates. Oh. Really? You think so? Hang on then.'

He covered the phone with his hand and turned to Anna.

'You're going to hate me,' he began, biting his lip, 'but Ruth's flying back to Barbados the day after tomorrow and there's this stuff she's been trying to sort out for me and she wants to meet up – of course, I'll say no because . . .'

'No, don't!' Anna protested. 'Honestly, it's fine. We can go out any time.'

The relief on his face told her she had said the right thing. 'You're sure? I wouldn't do this, only she and Joseph – that's her husband – they're flying off to do this research project in Patagonia in two weeks.'

'Go! It's fine, honestly. Just tell her!'

When he'd rung off, he turned to face her. 'You're amazing,' he said. 'Most girls would have sulked for England. Thanks, Anna – and I'll make it up to you. I promise.'

'I'll hold you to that,' she teased.

'In fact,' he said, pulling her towards him, 'I could start doing that right now.'

✂ CHAPTER 5 ✂

'Her regrets . . . clouded every enjoyment of youth.'
(Jane Austen, *Persuasion*)

ON THE HOTTEST DAY OF SUMMER SO FAR, THE ELIOTS moved out of Hampton House. The Crofts had been happy to pay the exorbitant rental that Walter was demanding on the proviso that they could move in speedily and be guaranteed at least a three-year tenure. Since Marina, ever the diplomat, had arranged for the Dalrymples to invite Walter to take part in a regatta at Eastbourne just days after his arrival at Sovereign Harbour, he made rather less fuss about it than might otherwise have been the case.

The Sovereign Harbour penthouse was very stylish and extremely spacious and, he was forced to admit, tastefully furnished; having agreed to leave the bulk of his own furniture at Hampton House rather than pay for it to go into storage, he was relieved that he wasn't going to be living, as he put it, 'with a lot of Ikea self-assembly stuff'. What's more, the apartment block stood on the prestigious Martello Quay, which, he was pleased to read in *Sussex Life*, was *quite the most elegant and well-positioned part of the development, in which several well-known theatrical personalities have second homes.*

As for his objections to Anna's decision to move in with Marina, they were non-existent; she had told him on the day they all went to view the new apartment, hoping that any ensuing argument might be softened by his desire not to show himself up in front of the new neighbours. In the event, he simply expressed relief that she would be nearby should 'darling Mallory' need her, and then expressed even more relief when Marina confirmed that she would take care of Anna's upkeep for as long as she was at Magpie Cottage.

'And,' he had said with ill-concealed glee, 'the room you would have had can be used as a guest room. I plan to entertain,' he added grandly.

They all knew precisely who, in particular, he was planning to entertain – and she wouldn't be using the guest room. Indeed, the fact that his agent, Araminta Clay, lived in Sussex had made the move to the coast a lot smoother than it might have been. Araminta had been his agent ever since the launch of his first chat show, and she had stuck by him ever since. She adored Walter and he adored being idolised. Neither Anna nor Mallory could stand the woman, but Gaby had always been cloyingly nice to her, because Araminta's daughter, Honeysuckle, was a successful model with one of the top London agencies and had promised to introduce Gaby to a couple of high-profile photographers.

When Araminta heard that Walter would actually be living just a half-hour drive away from her home in Lewes, she could hardly contain her excitement and had already promised him use of her season ticket to the opera at Glyndebourne, her beach hut on the Hove esplanade, and a few other things not verbalised but brazenly hinted at. Added to that, there were murmurs of a slot on *Coast TV* and even an autobiography ('Darling, it would sell like hot cakes, you're such a gem'). By the time the removal van drew up outside Hampton House, Walter had convinced himself that the whole idea of downsizing had been his own brilliant solution in the first place.

Anna was the last to leave the family home on the day of the move. Having spent the whole morning ferrying Mallory and a vast number of her possessions to Uppercross Farm, and stepping in every time her father's language to the removal men crossed the mark of polite behaviour, she hadn't had time to engage with her own feelings. Now, as the van disappeared down the drive, followed by Gaby in her bright-red MG, the realisation that this was it hit her in the middle of her chest like a bullet from a gun. She was due to set off for Marina's, but since she was too strung up to concentrate on driving, she decided to take one last look at the house and garden before she went.

As she was idly swinging on the old rope swing that still hung from one of the gnarled apple trees and thinking about her mum, she heard the crunch of tyres on the gravel followed by the slamming of a car door. Assuming that her sister had forgotten something, she ran across the lawn and round the side of the house.

And stopped dead in her tracks.

It wasn't Gaby.

It was Ruth Croft. She had a mobile phone clamped to

her ear and, from the horrified expression on her face, it was clear that whatever she was hearing was not good news.

For a second, Anna considered disappearing into the bushes that flanked the garden but, before she could move more than a couple of paces, she heard something that made her blood run cold and rooted her to the spot.

'A booby trap? Oh my God!'

In that instant, Anna knew what it was to feel sick with fear. It was Felix – it had to be. He'd been killed.

'He did what? How badly hurt?' Ruth's next words flooded Anna with relief for a brief instant, until an image of Felix lying mangled and bleeding at the roadside caused her to gag. Clamping her hand to her mouth, she edged nearer the driveway.

'He did? Speak up please, I can't hear . . . when?' Ruth had dropped her voice and Anna realised she was holding her breath as she strained to hear what she was saying. 'Is it . . .? Oh thank God.'

The siren from a passing police car blotted out any chance of catching the rest of her words and, by the time Anna crossed the drive to where her car was parked, she had rung off.

'Mrs Croft?'

Ruth spun round at the sound of Anna's voice.

'Oh my goodness, dear, you made me jump!' she cried, clearly startled. 'I'd thought you'd all left – your father said it would be OK.'

'The others have gone,' Anna assured her, alarmed to see a tear trickling down Ruth's face. 'I was just leaving.' She gestured to where her Smart car, still bearing the "P" plates from her newly passed driving test, was parked.

'Oh, that's all right then – Joseph's on his way following the removal men. I came ahead to open up and then the phone rang and . . .'

Anna could bear it no longer. 'Was it about Fe— your nephew?' she asked, hardly daring to breathe. 'I couldn't help overhearing – is he OK?'

'Thanks be to God, yes – it's a miracle. He's making light of it all but . . .'

'You spoke to him?' Anna couldn't restrain the eagerness in her voice.

Ruth nodded. 'Only for a moment or two, the connection was terrible. Let me tell you, when I took the call and a voice said it was Felix's commanding officer – well, you can imagine what I thought, and the relief when he put Felix on the line.'

Her voice cracked and Anna could see that her hands were shaking. 'I don't know all the details – apparently they were on patrol and a grenade went off. He hurled himself on to it to save the others.'

'Oh God.' Anna felt sick just thinking about it.

'And you know what?' Ruth said with a faint smile. 'His kitbag took most of the impact. He's deaf in one ear – they say that's temporary though; and he's got a torn ligament, lots of cuts and bruises, and a couple of broken fingers, but that's it.'

Her voice broke again, and she looked away, clearly embarrassed at her show of emotion. 'His guardian angel must have been working overtime,' she said when she had composed herself. 'According to the officer, the first thing he asked when the medics got to him was whether Zac was OK.'

'Zac?' The name stuck in Anna's throat. 'Zac Harville?'

'Yes, that's the one – they've been friends for years, really close they are. I met him once or twice when I was over in England. Lovely, gentle guy. Why, do you know him?'

'My sister went out with him for a bit,' she murmured. 'Is he OK?'

'I guess he must be,' said Ruth. 'All the officer said was that thanks to Felix's quick thinking, no one was seriously hurt.'

Despite dreading the fact that she would be recognised, Anna could see that Ruth was trembling and she felt compelled to help. 'Can I get you a glass of water or a coffee or something?' she ventured. 'We left a few supplies and there's some milk in the fridge.'

'That's sweet of you,' Ruth said. 'But no – I'm all right. Joseph will be here in a bit and I must try to get in touch with Felix's mother. She's on holiday – scuba-diving in Papua New Guinea, if you please – and they couldn't reach her.' She sighed. 'Between you and me, I don't get on with her. Frankly, I'll never know why my brother married her in the first place, and that's not because I'm racist or against mixed marriages or anything like that. Oh listen to me, babbling on. I do that when I'm upset, it drives Joseph mad.' She smiled wanly at Anna. 'She's not the maternal type, and Felix was always a daddy's boy as a kid. Then his father got ill and that really cut him up. He's always been a bit of a loner —'

'Does he have a girlfriend?' The words had spilled out before Anna had had a chance to stop herself. 'I mean, I wonder if she knows what's happened.'

'Well, there was a girl he seemed keen on. He emailed me

a photo once – funny-looking little thing with the strangest hair.'

Anna's hand went instinctively towards her head, and just as hastily away again. 'So what happened?' Her voice was shaky.

'It didn't last. I never found out why. We were in Patagonia for over a year you see, and half the time miles from anywhere – just a satellite phone once in a while. I asked a few questions, interfering auntie that I am, but he clammed up, wouldn't speak about her. He said she wasn't worth wasting his breath on.'

'I'm sorry, Mrs Croft, but I must be getting on,' Anna said, feeling the colour rushing to her face.

'Of course you must, dear,' Ruth nodded. 'Forgive me rabbiting on like that. As if it was of any interest to you.'

Anna smiled wanly and headed for the car.

'Now you just tell your father not to worry,' Ruth called after her. 'We'll look after this place like it was our own. And you must come over and meet Felix – lovely girl like you might be just what he needs to help him get over the shock of what's happened.'

'Bye, Mrs Croft.' Anna yanked open the car door and gave a half-hearted wave in Ruth's direction. Firing the engine, she shot off down the drive, spraying gravel in all directions. What a fool she had been to imagine that she could somehow put things straight, and even make Felix fall in love with her all over again. That was never going to happen. Once Felix knew that his aunt was living in Anna's old home, he would probably avoid the place like the plague; and even if he didn't, as soon Ruth discovered the truth, she would make sure that Anna didn't come within ten miles of him, never mind get an invitation to Hampton House.

He said she wasn't worth wasting his breath on. Ruth's words echoed in Anna's head as she stamped her foot on the accelerator and sped down the road towards Marina's village. But every turn in the road reminded her of things they had done and places they had walked. The tears that blinded her made her incapable of driving; she pulled off the road, lay her head on the steering wheel and sobbed until she made herself feel physically sick.

Ten minutes later, peering in the driving mirror and wiping the smudged mascara from her cheeks, she gave herself a firm talking to. What good, she demanded of her reflection, did it do to go over and over every detail? It only made matters worse. She blew her nose and was about to drive the short distance to Magpie Cottage, when her phone rang.

'Hi Shannon, how are you?'

'Better than you, obviously,' Shannon replied. 'You've been crying.'

'No, no – it's just hay fever.'

'Stop the bullshit,' Shannon replied amicably. 'So what's up?'

Knowing that there was no way that she could pull the wool over her friend's eyes for long, she gave her a shortened version of the morning's events.

'And so, that's that,' she concluded. 'As soon as Ruth finds out from Felix that I'm the girl that blew him out, and . . .'

'Hang on, hang on,' Shannon butted in. 'What's it got

to do with her? Like she's Felix's nanny or something?'

'No but . . .'

'Anna, you've got to stop letting other people run your life for you,' Shannon declared. 'There were only two people in the relationship – you and Felix. And OK, you don't know how he's going to feel – but now he's had a brush with death, maybe he'll be wanting to see you more than anything on earth.'

Anna gave a short laugh. 'You always were a romantic,' she said.

'Better that than a pessimist,' her friend replied. 'Now I've had the best idea.'

'Not another one of your schemes,' said Anna.

'It just came to me and it's the best yet,' replied Shannon, totally unfazed. 'Felix is coming back and he's bound to stay with his aunt, right? So how about we work it so Wild Chicks get a slot to play at the Kellynch Festival? The cream teas are always in your – well, theirs now I guess – garden and he'd be bound to spot you.'

'Oh no, the Festival!' Anna gasped. 'I'd forgotten all about that.'

The two-day Kellynch Festival and Fayre was an ancient tradition dating back centuries and people came from miles around to share in it. There was something for everyone: charity polo matches and horse show and gymkhana in the grounds of the nearby agricultural college attracted the county set; the Barn Theatre provided the music and art venues, and the neighbourhood gardens, Hampton House among them, hosted cream teas, craft stalls, Punch and Judy and face painting for children. The whole weekend culminated in a comic chariot race and fun run in aid of charity.

'But your dad will have sorted it with the Crofts, right?'

'I doubt it,' Anna replied ruefully. 'He's had rather a lot on his mind. I bet you the Crofts know nothing about it.'

'So tell them,' Shannon said. 'I've already phoned Mia and Lauren and they're up for it.'

Anna's mind was racing. 'Look, Marina's bound to know what's going on – she's the one who sorted all the details out with the tenants. I'll check it out with her, OK?'

'Brilliant,' Shannon said. 'Because if this plan doesn't work, I'll come up with something else. One way or another, Felix Wentworth is going to fall in love with you all over again before the summer's out.'

'Hi Marina! It's me!'

Anna staggered through the front door, which had been wedged open with a wrought-iron doorstop in the shape of a horse's head, and dumped the last of her bags on the stone floor. Delightful and Delicious, Marina's two blue Burmese cats, stalked out of the kitchen towards her, mewing demandingly and eyeing her with the contempt that only that breed can muster.

'Marina?'

Anna pushed the door open and stepped into the low-ceilinged sitting room with its ancient beams and inglenook fireplace.

On the opposite wall was Marina's new plasma TV, in front of which her godmother stood rooted to the spot, gazing at the footage on the screen: armoured vehicles throwing up clouds of dust, Marines in desert fatigues carrying weapons over their shoulders, and then the words of the unseen newsreader.

'*The Marines from 45 Commando are being flown home to RAF Lyneham . . . commander praised the swift and selfless action of Second Lt. Felix Wentworth . . . prevented a far greater disaster. Second Lt Wentworth threw himself . . .*'

It was at that moment that Marina heard Anna's footsteps on the stone floor. She turned, gasped and reached instantly for the remote control.

'Don't bother, I already know.' Anna couldn't keep the note of anger out of her voice. Why did everyone tread so carefully around the issue of her and Felix? Treat any mention of the past as if they were delving back into something murky and sordid?

'You know? How come?' Marina looked both embarrassed and anxious.

'I heard it on the car radio,' Anna lied. 'If I hadn't turned up right then, you wouldn't have said a word about it, would you?'

Marina came over and rested a hand on her shoulder, her tone softening. 'No darling, in all honesty, I wouldn't. What would have been the point? It's over, in the past, all that nasty business. And now that you're over your crush . . .'

'How dare you call it that?' All Anna's pent-up emotions, all the months of being the good daughter, the obedient one, spilled over in a waterfall of words. 'I loved him – I still do. I miss him like hell, and I know now that I should never, ever have listened to you and Dad. You used Mummy's memory to persuade me – and she'd never have wanted me to be so miserable!'

Anna was amazed at her own courage. Confrontation

was something she normally avoided at all costs.

'Now come on, sweetheart, that's just not true,' Marina replied briskly, turning her attention to re-arranging a perfectly tidy pile of magazines on the coffee table. 'She wanted the very best for you, and Felix and that mother of his were not it.'

'I wasn't going out with his mother,' Anna protested.

'Look, don't let's rake all that up again,' Marina urged. 'What's done is done.'

'And did you honestly think I wouldn't have found out about what's happened? I do watch the news, you know.'

Marina sighed and nodded. 'Oh, I know you would in time – I guess I just wanted to protect you. It's been a difficult day for you, the move and . . .'

'Protect me? Is that what you thought you were doing last year?'

Marina nodded again. 'And I still do. And while we're on the subject . . .' She gestured to Anna to sit down on the ample sofa overlooking the garden, and sank down beside her. 'The new tenants of Hampton House,' she continued. 'I know who they are.'

'Yes, you said,' Anna replied swiftly, her heart banging in her chest. 'She's an artist and he's writing a book.'

'Anna, give me some credit. I asked a few questions after you ran off in such a state. She's Felix Wentworth's aunt.'

'And I suppose you couldn't wait to tell Dad?'

'I haven't said a word to your father. I wanted to be sure the paperwork was all in place and he couldn't back out of the deal,' Marina assured her.

'Thank you,' Anna said.

'Oh, I didn't do it for you,' her godmother told her. 'I did it because your father needs to get an income from that house as fast as possible or he will go under. Even you don't know the true extent of the financial mess he's got himself into.' She took Anna's hand. 'Now listen, darling, you're older now and more mature, and I'm sure you can see how right your father and I were to persuade you to break off that rather unfortunate relationship.'

'Unfortunate for who, exactly?' Anna struggled to contain her anger.

'You,' Marina said shortly. 'You were so young, and he was – well, from such a different background, different lifestyle – and then, of course, with the way his mother behaved . . .'

'That was hardly his fault.'

'And it's not your father's fault that he wants better things for you,' Marina said firmly. 'So if Felix does visit his aunt – not that it's likely now, and I'm sure it will only be a fleeting visit because a young man won't want to hang around with a couple of old fogies for his entire leave – well, just don't go getting any silly ideas.'

'I won't,' Anna smiled wanly. Getting back with Felix didn't in her book qualify as a remotely silly idea.

'That's my girl – never look back, that's my motto,' Marina urged. 'Think about the future – a lovely summer ahead of you, and then off to uni in Exeter. You'll meet lots of nice boys there, and one day you'll find someone who will love you as you deserve to be loved. Someone who fits in with our way of life. Set your sights on all that.'

Anna gave a half smile. Of course, Marina wasn't aware that she'd originally chosen Exeter University for the simple reason that it was as close as she could get to where

Felix would be based once he passed out. But her godmother was right about one thing: it was the future that mattered. Felix was coming home and she had one last chance to put things straight. Keeping Marina in the dark as to her intentions was more important than winning this particular argument.

'Yes, that's true,' she sighed, with what she hoped was just the right amount of apology in her voice. 'What's done is done. And thanks so much for letting me stay here. You know, with the band and everything . . .'

The meekness of her tone had the desired effect.

'You're welcome, darling,' her godmother said, giving her a hug. 'I knew you'd see things my way. And, although I wasn't certain at first, maybe this band of yours is a good thing. Keep your mind occupied.'

She leaned back on the cushions with an air of satisfaction. 'Now, let's talk about more cheerful matters, shall we?'

'Actually,' Anna said, biting her tongue. 'I wanted to ask you about the village Festival. I mean, will the Crofts still open up the garden?'

'All sorted,' Marina declared. 'Actually, they're frightfully keen. I think they see it as a way of getting to know people. And Ruth seems a jolly, outgoing sort of soul. I suppose those West Indian sorts are.'

'That is such a stereotype . . .' Anna began, but Marina was in full flood.

'Sadly, I'll be in Madeira on my gardening society's annual trip – but of course Bea Musgrove's on the committee and she'll take the Crofts under her wing, make sure they know what's expected of them.'

Anna cringed inwardly at the patronising tone of Marina's voice but continued to smile sweetly.

'I know it will be agony for you to go, darling,' Marina went on, 'but I spoke to your father, and he said he'd be glad if you could just manage to pop in for an hour or so, just to fly the family flag and all that.' She paused. 'And I'm sure the nephew won't be there,' she murmured half to herself.

'Sure,' Anna smiled serenely. 'No problem at all. In fact, I'll look forward to it.'

An hour later, unpacking in the privacy of the large, under-eaves bedroom that Marina had assured her was hers for as long as she needed it, the full impact of the long day hit Anna with all the force of a runaway train. She felt exhausted – drained, emotionally and physically. Her home was in the hands of someone else; nothing would ever be the same again. Her sisters might kid themselves that they'd be back in Hampton House in a few years, but Anna knew that in reality it would take a miracle for her father to recoup all his financial losses.

So where was home now? Certainly not the apartment in Eastbourne – not yet at any rate – and lovely though it was, obviously not Marina's cottage. Suddenly she remembered a little stone plaque that her grandmother used to have hanging in her kitchen.

Home, it read, *is where the heart is*.

Her heart was where it had been every day since she had first met him. With Felix. She loved her family, infuriating as they could be – but she had to admit that, with them, she had always played the role they'd given her; she was the helpful, bookish, slightly timid one who hated confrontation and was good at sorting out other people's messes. Why did she do that, she thought angrily. Why was she so willing to let other people decide what was best for her?

She stuffed a pile of T-shirts into one of the dressing table drawers and wandered over to the window. Gazing out over the neighbouring fields, the thought that had so often niggled at her from the back of her mind reared its ugly head again.

Had Felix really loved her the way she had loved him? And, if he had, why hadn't he answered any of her emails or texts in the weeks following the break up? She had begged for a second chance – but he clearly hadn't been interested. Why?

Then, as clearly as if he was standing in the room beside her, his words echoed in her head.

'It's not going to work, Anna. You're never going to put us first – you'll always let someone else tell you what to do.'

Well, he was wrong about one thing. She wasn't always going to do that. Not any more. With a bit of luck, Felix would be staying with Ruth within a week or two – but for how long? This time she had to act and act decisively if she was ever going to put right the mess she had allowed to happen.

Sighing impatiently, she turned away from the window, her mind bombarded with hundreds of thoughts and memories. Exactly when did it all start to go wrong? Was it that fateful TV programme? Or before that, when Anna unwittingly played straight into the hands of Felix's manipulative mother? Suddenly it felt imperative that she should get it all completely clear in her head; because she had to make sure that she did things very differently this time round.

Abandoning the rest of her unpacking, she grabbed the battered tapestry holdall that had once belonged to her mother, the holdall in which she had hurled all her journals. She'd started keeping a diary during the dark days of her mum's last illness, and emptying her soul between the safe covers of a book was a habit she had kept up ever since.

Kicking off her sandals, she flopped down on the bed and emptied the journals on to the duvet. She picked up the bright pink one that she had started the week she met Felix and began flicking through the pages. She skim-read the entries about ice-skating on the flooded courtyard of Fleckford Castle, the films they'd seen (or rather not seen much of because they were too busy kissing one another), the days when they'd driven to Norfolk and walked for miles on Holkham beach. Then she paused at the entry for the beginning of April and, taking a deep breath, she began to read.

❧ CHAPTER 6 ❧

*'She had been forced into prudence in her youth, she learned
romance as she grew older: the natural sequence of an
unnatural beginning.'*
(Jane Austen, *Persuasion*)

EVERYTHING HAD HAPPENED SO FAST. FELIX AND ZAC HAD
both been accepted for Commando Training with the
Royal Marines and had been on a real high for days. Anna
had tried her hardest to be pleased for him, but when she
discovered that he'd be away for thirty-two weeks with
only a couple of breaks, she felt as if someone had stuck a
knife through her chest.

'Hey, don't look so sad,' he had said. 'We can email and
phone and, anyway, three weeks after we begin, families
get to come and suss out what we're up to – spend the day
and all that. You'll come, right?'

'But I'm not family.'

'I want you there. And they let girlfriends come – I
checked!'

He wants me there. I'm his girlfriend. Anna had hung
on to those words, repeating them to herself like a mantra.

* * *

'I think it's high time I met this black guy you're hanging out with.'

Walter and the girls, along with Marina and Araminta (who happened to be 'just passing' – something she did amazingly frequently considering she lived ninety miles away), were just finishing supper when Walter mentioned this.

'Why do you keep on about his colour?' Anna demanded, flicking cracker crumbs off the new dress she had bought for Leo Hayter's party. 'You didn't refer to Zac as "that white guy", did you?'

'That's different, he was . . .'

'His mum's white,' Anna went on. 'She's really into good causes and stuff. And she's standing for parliament. '

Even as she spoke, she despised herself for immediately going on the defensive. What did it matter what colour his mother was or what she did or didn't do? Except that she knew her father always warmed to high profile people.

'Really?' Araminta was all attention. 'What's her name?'

'Cassandra Wentworth,' Anna said. 'Dad wanted her on his show once.'

'The Wentworth woman?' Walter burst out, pouring himself another glass of pinot noir. 'The one who refused to do a slot with me? Self-opinionated —'

'Heavens above!' Araminta gasped. 'Now there's a thing. Where's she standing?'

'Muckleborough and Bythorn,' Anna replied. 'Why?'

'You should get your producer on to this one right now,' Araminta declared, turning to Walter. 'She'll be desperate for publicity now and you could do a really hard-hitting slot.'

'What? Give her air time when she refused before? Who do you take me for?'

'Darling,' Araminta cooed, her steely gaze belying the softness of her words. 'I take you for someone who has been blanked by the Beeb, who has lost a prime-time slot and whose ratings are dropping like the proverbial stone. Nothing to do with you of course, angel, it's the programmers who need a rocket up their . . . well, anyway, get Cassandra W on the show . . . It could be interesting, and she might produce some headline-hitting stuff.'

'Worth a try, I suppose,' Walter nodded. 'I am exceedingly good at the head-on confrontation.'

He smiled around at everyone as if waiting for a round of applause.

'Anyway,' he went on when it wasn't forthcoming, 'that can wait. Right now, I want to meet this chap, Anna. Gaby's not at all sure he's our type – and certainly his mother's a bit of a rough diamond if I recall – ghastly accent and the dress sense of a . . . good grief, what's that?' Walter stopped in mid sentence as the sound of a blaring car horn shattered the peace.

'Oh – er, that'll just be my friends. They said they'd pick me up on the way to the party,' Anna gabbled, glaring at Gaby who had the good grace to look mildly embarrassed.

'And this Felix – he's out there, is he?' Walter interrupted. 'Well, for goodness' sake, bring him in and let's give him the once over.'

'Not now, Dad, not with everyone here.'

'Everyone? Everyone? These are our dear friends,' Walter boomed, moving into his on-screen persona and smiling magnanimously at Marina and Araminta. 'Now come along, we'll move into the sitting room – can't have guests in this chaos!' He ushered them out of the kitchen, allowing his hand briefly to caress Araminta's backside as he did so. 'Now for goodness' sake, go and fetch him, if only to stop that confounded horn blasting away!'

It wasn't how Anna had planned the first meeting between her father and Felix. In truth, she hadn't really planned it at all – in fact, she had done all in her power to avoid it. It was all so new, this feeling of being in love, and she didn't want anything or anybody to spoil it. The confrontational style that made her father famous wasn't so entertaining off-screen, and she knew that, deep down, he was a snob with very definite views on whom to include in the circle he liked his family to move in.

And the fact was, that much as she hated to admit it even to herself, Felix wasn't like the other boys that her father was used to having hanging round the house. He wasn't public school and he didn't shoot game, or sail or ride.

She would just have to hope that, if her dad wanted to get Cassandra on the show, he'd suck up to Felix big time. Clearly, his agent was thinking along the same lines.

'I just love meeting young people, don't you, Walt?' she could hear Araminta coo. 'Of course, I have terrific empathy with them, and I'm sure this Felix lad will take to me, so if you just let me chat him up . . .'

Rather than vomit on the spot, Anna left her to go on, resigning herself to the inevitable. After all, how bad could it be? A quick hello and a drink and they'd be off. And that would be that.

Only it hadn't quite worked out like that. When Anna

opened the front door, she found not just one car parked there but two. Jamie Benwick was at the wheel of the VW Polo that his parents had given him on his eighteenth, with Phoebe, Zac's sister, sitting at his side.

'Reinforcements,' Felix grinned, giving Anna a kiss. 'Phoebe's taken pity on Zac!'

'Got tired of his moping, more like,' Phoebe laughed, climbing out of the car and flicking a solitary strand of bright pink hair behind her ear. (Phoebe was experimenting with new looks and it occurred to Anna that the current one was not an unqualified success.) 'Give me five minutes, and Gaby will be putty in Zac's hands.'

I wouldn't count on it, Anna thought, but decided to say nothing.

'So where is she?' Zac asked. It was at times like these, when Zac acted like a lovesick fourteen-year-old, that Anna found it hard to imagine him facing an enemy under gunfire. Although, on second thoughts, she reasoned, facing Gaby would be perfect practice.

'In the sitting room but you see . . .'

'OK, let's get her!' Phoebe cried. 'We get her to the party and then it's up to you! God, I just hope she's worth it.' With that, she and Jamie hurried into the house, eagerly followed by Zac.

'Wait!' Anna grabbed Felix's arm. 'Dad wants to meet you.'

'That's cool,' Felix replied. 'What's the problem?'

'It's just that – well, you know – he's a bit, well you know . . . I mean, you will be . . . I mean, don't mind if . . .'

'Anna, you are not making any sense,' he laughed. 'Suppose I just go and find out for myself?'

Whatever Phoebe had said to Gaby clearly worked; by the time Anna and Felix were through the front door, she was dashing upstairs to change, followed by Phoebe who gave the thumbs up to a flushed but exuberant-looking Zac.

'Phoebe let slip that Zac's got tickets for the *Hi5* concert at the MK Bowl next week,' Felix muttered in Anna's ear as they lingered in the hall. 'That'll be the reason for your sister's sudden change of heart – nothing to do with poor old Zac.'

Anna was about to reply when her father burst out of the sitting room, an expression of forced friendliness on his face.

'Well now, so you're the mysterious Felix?' His eyes travelled from the top of Felix's head to the toes of his scuffed trainers and back again. 'Glad to meet you. Wine? Lager?'

'No thanks, I'm driving,' Felix said. 'But if you've got a lemonade, that'd be cool.'

'Sensible, sensible – good man!' Anna prayed that it was only she who had noticed her father's slight wince at Felix's accent. 'Anna, get him a drink. Now come and meet my agent, Araminta Clay, and our dear friend, Marina Russell.'

Walter continued to be charm personified for the first five minutes, using all his finely honed techniques for putting interviewees at their ease and then suddenly switched into interrogation mode, launching into a battery of questions about Felix's schooling ('State school all the way through? Well, I suppose someone has to – ha! Ha!'), his hobbies ('Climbing and potholing? Not very sociable pursuits, are they?') and where he lived ('Fleckford? Lovely town . . . Oh, *East* Fleckford. Ah.')

'And your parents? Of course, I know a bit about your mother, although not as much as I would had she had the sense to come on my show.'

Anna could sense Felix becoming defensive.

'Hey, we ought to be heading off,' she said hastily, making a big show of looking at her watch. 'Leo's parties always get going really quickly and . . .'

'A feisty woman, as I recall from the press cuttings. And Anna tells me she now has political aspirations?' Walter continued, ignoring Anna completely. 'Fascinating – Labour, I take it?' A slight flaring of his nostrils showed his view of socialists generally and the current government in particular.

'Independent, actually,' Felix replied. 'She thinks party politics have been the downfall of this country.'

'Really? Extraordinary. And your father? Wentworth doesn't sound – well, an African sort of name.'

If there was an award for embarrassing parents, Anna thought, her father would win it hands down.

'That's because my dad is Jamaican,' Felix replied, breathing deeply which, as Anna had come to recognise, was a sign that he was working very hard at not being rude. 'Way back, when my great great – oh, I can't remember how many greats – grandfather was a slave, he belonged to the Wentworth plantation. That's how he got the surname.'

'My dear, how fascinating,' Araminta enthused. 'Slaves. What an interesting family. And you? Gabriella tells us you're joining the Marines.'

Felix nodded. 'Yes, Zac and I are off to start our training soon.'

'Your family must be so proud of you,' Marina remarked.

'Defence of the realm and all that.'

'Use your brain, Marina,' Walter interjected. 'I doubt his mother's over the moon about it – she's spent her life being extremely vocal about that very topic.'

'We really must get going,' Anna stressed, seizing Felix's hand.

'But your father?' Araminta queried.

'Anna, we really have to go.' Felix turned to her, a pleading look in his eyes.

Then Walter slapped him on the back, said how delightful it had been to meet him and how he must feel free to call round any time he wanted – and Anna instantly forgave him for all his blustering. He approved, which was all that mattered, and from now on everything was going to be plain sailing. She might not have spent the rest of the evening on such a high, had she heard Araminta's murmured aside to Walter as she and Felix went in search of the others.

'Well, well, well. Your Anna hooking up with the son of Cassandra Wentworth. Oh Walter, we're going to take advantage of this one.'

'What? Anna and some black guy from the wrong side of Fleckford? Are you insane?'

'Bear with it, just for a while. Trust me, it'll be worth it,' Araminata replied firmly. 'I seem to recall a rumour that . . . Well, anyway, there's a story worth telling there, you mark my words. And if I have anything to do with it, it's going to be *Walt at the Weekend* that breaks it.'

It had been a couple of days afterwards that they'd had their first major row. They'd been walking to the cinema and Anna had asked Felix what his dad did.

'Not a lot,' he had replied abruptly.

'So where does he live? Do you see a lot of him?' she'd asked. 'Will I meet him at Families Day?'

'Anna, for God's sake, drop it, will you?' Felix burst out, letting go of her hand and turning to face her. 'What is all this? Checking us out, are you? Making sure we're good enough for you and your county-set family?'

Anna's stomach began churning. Any other time, she would have let the matter drop, but she was feeling totally hormonal and so edgy that she felt she might explode at any moment. And what if this was his way of saying he was going off her? What if he wanted to cool things, to go away to his training and forget her?

'I'm just interested that's all,' she muttered. 'You've met my family and I just thought it would be great to . . .'

'I've had it with this conversation,' Felix shouted, dropping her hand. 'You know what? Forget this evening. You're clearly far more worried about getting the low-down on my folks than you are about being with me.'

'That's not true . . .'

'So what's with all this family get-together stuff? Seems a bit full on to me.'

'OK – I won't say another word . . .'

'Say as many as you like, because I'm not hanging around to hear them!'

He turned and strode off, stopping suddenly and walking back towards her.

'Here.' He thrust a ten-pound note into her hand.

'What's that?' Anna muttered, choking back tears.

'Taxi fare home,' he grunted. 'I'm hardly going to leave

you stranded in the middle of Fleckford on a Saturday night, am I?'

And with that he turned round and walked away without a backward glance.

The next forty-eight hours were hell. He didn't phone, he didn't text, and he didn't email. At night, Anna dreamed that he was shouting at her and telling her to get lost; each day she wrote loads of texts and deleted them all. And she didn't really understand what she'd done wrong. She'd obviously irritated him – but how?

The text when it came was brief.

Things we need to sort. Meet me in Kellynch Woods 6 p.m. this evening? F x

The tension had been palpable to start with. As they walked down one of the narrow footpaths that led deep into the woods, their conversation had been almost monosyllabic.

'You OK?'

'I guess.'

'School OK?'

'Mmm.'

'Shall we go this way?'

'If you like.'

'Shall we sit here?'

'Sure.'

And then suddenly, as they sat down side by side on a fallen log, they were both speaking at once.

'Look, about Saturday, I should never have suggested . . .'

'I was out of order . . .'

'I promise I won't ever . . .'

'I was totally out of order,' Felix confessed, laying a

finger on her lips to silence her. 'I want to tell you everything. Except it's hard to know how.'

He paused chewing his lip and avoiding her eyes.

'When your mum was ill, I guess your dad took care of her, right?' he asked.

Anna nodded. 'Well yes – I mean, Macmillan nurses came in each day and eventually she went to a hospice, but she wanted to be at home for as long as she could and . . .'

'Precisely!' Felix thumped his fist on to the log. 'She wanted to be at home and your dad made sure it happened. So – you wanted to know why I was in such a foul mood? It's because of what my mum has done to my dad.'

'Go on.'

'Dad's a lot older than Mum – sixteen years actually. And he idolised her.'

Anna noted the past tense but thought it best to stay silent.

'He did everything he could to make her happy. Stayed at home with me so that she could work, bought her everything she wanted, fielded all the media stuff when she did something stupid. And she was all over him, because it suited her. But then, a couple of years back, he got ill.'

Anna didn't know what to say. She knew the agonies and the grief she'd gone through when her mum was sick.

'I didn't want to go off on my gap year trip because of it, but Mum said I should, and Dad, well, he wasn't too bad then. He made a joke about it, and he was really keen for me to go to South America. He kept telling me to go and have fun. So I did. I'll never forgive myself.'

'Why?'

'Because, by the time I got back, my mother had put him in a home.'

His voice cracked with emotion and he turned away, picked a stick up from the ground and hurled it into the surrounding bushes.

'A home? But I don't understand.'

Felix took a deep breath, swallowed hard and looked at her straight in the eyes. 'My dad's sixty-eight,' he said, 'and he's got Alzheimer's disease. In the six months I was away, he went downhill so fast that, by the time I got home, he didn't even know who I was.'

Anna had sat and listened as it all spilled out – how he blamed his mother for not caring for his dad at home, how he thought politics meant more to her than her own husband.

'I am just so angry about the whole thing. Dad deserves better; he was the one I could depend on when I was growing up, you see. My sister went off to work in America, and Oscar was rarely home, but Dad was always there. Mum on the other hand was always disappearing on some protest or mission. Greenham, Faslane – you name it she was there. Me and Dad, we were like a team.'

He picked at a piece of loose bark on the log. 'I'm sorry I went off on one last Saturday, though,' he admitted, standing up and pulling Anna to her feet.

'I was worried when I didn't hear from you,' Anna replied.

'I was going to phone and then you know what? On Sunday, Mum announces that actually she's not going to come with me to see Dad that day after all because there's some meeting of Churches Together in Fleckford and she reckons it'll do her profile good to be seen there. Can you believe it? Parading at church, pretending to be holier than thou . . .' He kicked the trunk of a nearby tree.' . . . just because it looked good – hypocritical or what? So I went on my own.'

'And . . .?'

Felix shook his head. 'He looks like my dad but it's not him any more. He can't keep track of a conversation and when you mention people he's known for years, he just stares at you blankly. He's got much worse since he's been in the home. It wouldn't have happened so fast if he'd been with us.'

Anna felt it best to say nothing.

'Anyway,' Felix went on, 'let's not talk about it any more, OK? We've only got a short time before I'll be going away. Let's make the most of it. Just the two of us.'

And despite the fact that Anna was up to her eyes in revision for AS-levels, they had. When the holidays ended, she got up at five every morning to work so that she could meet Felix after school; and she even skived off in the middle of the day – something that not even Sixth Formers were allowed to do unless by what the Head called 'prior arrangement under extenuating circumstances'. Of course, the circumstances were extenuating; time with Felix was running out. She hated the thought that he would be gone – but had to admit that she quite enjoyed being something of a celebrity, especially since for once it had nothing to do with her father. The fact that Felix met her at the school gates most days and sent her emails and texts heavy with double meaning gave her instant street cred and fascination value.

'That is one sexy guy,' Shannon commented. 'If you weren't my mate, I'd fight you for him!'

'So when's he going away?' Lauren asked pointedly. 'I'd like to know so I can prepare for your moping about, you know stock up on tissues and stuff!'

That day came all too quickly. They'd agreed to meet for one last time at the crack of dawn that morning down by Kellynch Lake, before Felix met up with Zac and headed off to Lympstone and Anna went to school.

'I love you, Anna,' he had whispered, his lips caressing her neck and brushing across her cheek. 'I've never felt like this about anyone before.'

'And I love you too,' she had murmured, her whole body quivering as he pulled her towards him.

'Don't cry,' he said, knotting her scarf more tightly round her neck as she shivered in the chill breeze. 'Remember, it's only three weeks till Families Day. You will come? Promise?'

'Just you try stopping me,' she had replied. 'I'll be counting the days.'

And then he had pulled her down on to the grass under a canopy of newly budding ash and beech trees, and kissed her with a hunger and intensity that sent shivers of electricity through her body.

'Don't forget me,' he mumbled, his voice thick with emotion.

'I never will, never ever,' she replied.

And that, she thought now, was one promise she had never broken.

CHAPTER 7

'There is nothing so bad as separation . . .'
(Jane Austen, *Persuasion*)

THE THREE WEEKS BETWEEN FELIX LEAVING AND ANNA going to see him at Lympstone had been agony. Anna had tried to lose herself in her school work and music, but whatever she did and wherever she went, Felix was in her mind twenty-four seven. For the first couple of days, his texts had been full of how many press ups he'd done and how he was learning close quarter combat, but then the messages got shorter and shorter, till by the end of the second week all she got was *Speed march today – too tired to speak* and, on a couple of occasions, she got no text at all.

'Don't worry,' Phoebe had reassured her when Anna confessed that she was worried that Felix wasn't missing her at all. 'Zac's just the same – Mum sends him loads of texts and all she gets back is, *All OK here*. I guess there's no chance of Gaby coming down for Families Day,' she ventured.

Anna shook her head. She had tried to persuade her, because Felix had said that Zac still missed her like crazy. For once, Gaby had been honest with Anna.

'I can't do it,' she had admitted. 'I mean, it was a bit of a laugh, and he was fun to hang out with – like concerts and parties and stuff; but I can't get all heavy about it. I can't do all the waiting at home, and worrying myself sick about him. And besides, you know what? I met this boy at Sophie's party – he works for *Zing!* magazine and that's much more me than all this war stuff.'

So, in the end, Anna had travelled to Lympstone with Mrs Harville and Phoebe. Felix had told her that no one else from his family was coming – his father obviously couldn't, his brother and sister led their own lives now, and his mother just wasn't interested. Mrs Harville hated driving long distances and so they went by train. Most of the journey was taken up with Phoebe dithering about whether to ditch Jamie ('He is just *too* good and *too* nice') or stick with him till the summer because his family were hinting that they might take her to their house in Umbria in August. When she wasn't talking about Jamie, she was arguing with her mother who had been unwise enough to comment that she wished Phoebe had put on a nice dress like Anna, to which Phoebe replied that jeans were just fine for Families Day and no way was she going to dress up and look like an over-iced cupcake. That made Anna worry that she had overdone it, but when they changed on to the branch line at Exeter, they found themselves surrounded by lots of anxious-looking parents, chattering children and several girls like herself, all dressed in their posh dresses and all trying to look nonchalant and laid-back – but clearly as keyed up and excited as Anna was.

And then they were there, and Felix was waiting for her and they kissed with the kind of eager desperation that comes from wanting time to stand still and the moment never to end. Anna closed her eyes, breathing in the musky smell of him and relishing the way he gently swept the hair back from her face and kissed her eyelids, her cheeks, her lips . . .

'It's so good to see you,' he murmured, as Zac dragged his mum and sister off. 'Look, there are a load of displays and stuff, and then later on, a talk all about how they look after us, and what happens when we get deployed – but really you don't have to . . .'

'I want to go,' Anna said firmly. 'I want to know every last detail about what's happening to you.'

Catching the fleeting look of gratitude on his face, she took a deep breath. 'Is it hard – I mean, with all this going on around you?' She gestured to the groups of parents hugging their sons. 'Your mum not being here, I mean?'

He shook his head. 'Don't go there,' he said with a slight edge to his voice. 'You're here and that's what matters.'

'Well, I've got a surprise for you,' Anna told him, fingering the tickets for the *Sugar Lumps* New Year concert at the O$_2$ that she blown her monthly allowance on. 'Do you want it now or . . .?'

'Later,' Felix grinned. 'Come on, let me show you round and then you can watch what it's really like to be in training!'

Half an hour later, Anna was standing in the sunshine, watching Felix and several other recruits attempt the assault course. The instructor acting as their guide pointed out the obstacles while others yelled encouragement – and occasionally expletives – at those taking part. Felix had tackled the swing bridge and the gate vault and was running towards the ten-metre wall when he stumbled to his knees.

'Come on, Felix, go, go, go!' A sharp-featured, fair-haired woman in a scarlet coat and black knee-length boots elbowed her way in front of Anna, craning her neck as Felix, panting hard, staggered to his feet and began scaling the wall.

'Yes!' The woman punched the air with both hands and Anna was aware of flash bulbs going off behind her. Just then, the woman turned and looked at Anna apologetically. 'Sorry, I didn't mean to barge in front of you – just that, seeing my son . . .'

'Your son? You mean – oh! You're Cassandra Wentworth!' Anna gasped. 'But Felix said you weren't coming?' The words were out before she'd had the chance to think.

'What do you mean, Felix said . . . Oh my goodness! Don't tell me you're the new girlfriend he's been going on about?' She peered at Anna through heavily mascaraed eyelashes in much the same way as one might examine an exhibit in a museum. 'So you're this paragon of female perfection!' she commented with wry amusement. 'The girl who is everything his mother is not.'

'I – er – I'm sure he'll be over the moon that you're here,' Anna mumbled, hardly knowing how to respond.

'I doubt it,' his mother replied equably, glancing down the assault course where Felix was nearing the last obstacle. 'At the moment, I can't do anything right in his eyes. It was wrong that I didn't want to come, and now I've turned up you can bet that'll be wrong too.' She pulled a face. 'I guess that's the price one pays for motherhood,' she murmured.

Anna thought she made being a mum sound like a

particularly nasty dose of flu. She also knew she should be pleased that Cassandra had decided to show up but in reality she was furious; she could hardly snog Felix with his mother hovering in the background and it would be weeks until she saw him again.

'He told me you're standing for Parliament,' Anna said, trying to get on to safer ground.

'That's right!' Cassandra became very animated. 'You see before you the Independent candidate for Muckleborough and Bythorn.'

'So you think you'll oust the Lib Dems?' Anna commented. 'But surely the Conservatives look set fair to . . .'

'Not since their candidate blotted his copybook with that rather sleazy moment in Corfu,' Cassandra muttered. 'Not to mention the first-class flights and chauffeur-driven limo courtesy of the taxpayer. But . . . are you telling me you're interested in politics? Felix never said. Mind you, Felix never says much these days. So – how do you feel about this crazy idea of his?'

'What? Wanting to join the Marines?'

Cassandra nodded. 'So you think it's crazy?' she asked.

'No, what I meant was . . . well, of course, if I'm selfish, I wish he'd chosen another career . . . but on the other hand . . .'

'Of course you do.' Cassandra nodded. 'And you haven't been able to dissuade him?'

'I didn't try,' Anna replied. 'I mean, if this is what really gets him going, makes him happy . . .'

'But what about your relationship? I mean, do you see you two having a future together?'

Anna was feeling more and more uncomfortable. If she

said yes, she'd sound too eager, and if she said no, she'd be lying.

'I don't know – I mean, we only got together a few months ago, and we're young. Who knows? It depends what happens . . .'

'What'll happen is that he'll be sent off to some remote corner of the globe to kill people,' Cassandra said emphatically. 'Doesn't that bother you?'

'Well, yes, of course – I mean war's awful and I know I could never shoot someone, but on the other hand, if people like Felix weren't prepared to . . .'

'Oh look – here he comes,' Cassandra butted in. 'Time for a change of subject, I think.'

As he drew closer, dodging the clusters of onlookers, Felix caught sight of his mother. He stood stock-still, staring at her open-mouthed.

'Surprised to see me, darling?' She went up to him and planted a dainty kiss on his cheek. 'Thought for a moment back there that you were going to fall flat on your face. So good on you for —'

'I tripped, that's all,' he retorted, eyeing her suspiciously, turning to Anna. 'So this is your surprise?'

'No,' Anna said, without thinking. 'As if I would do that, knowing . . .' She checked herself just in time. 'I've only this minute met your mum.'

'Oh. Sorry. Anyway, why are you here, Mum?'

'It's Families Day, Felix,' Cassandra replied. 'And I'm family.'

'You swore you wouldn't come. So what's changed?'

'Darling, I may not agree with what you're doing but I do care about your welfare. I wanted to see where you're based, what's in store, all that sort of thing. And it's lovely to meet Anna,' she concluded, giving her a glittering smile and patting her arm.

'Yeah, well . . . you'd better come and see my quarters,' he replied grudgingly, slipping his hand into Anna's and gripping it tightly.

For a minute or two they walked in silence towards the accommodation block.

'So how was Dad last weekend?' Felix asked suddenly, turning to face his mother.

'Well, I didn't see him . . .'

'Don't tell me,' Felix cut in, 'you didn't go? You're unbelievable!'

'I didn't see him last weekend because I had a bug and that's the last thing he needs,' Cassandra said firmly.

Felix had the good grace to look embarrassed.

'But Oscar went and said he was much the same as usual. One of the carers said he is still trying to wander off.'

'Like, maybe he wants to go home?' Felix snapped.

'Felix, we've been over this a hundred times,' Cassandra replied. 'It hurts me as much as it hurts you, but having him back is simply not an option. He needs specialist care.'

She touched Felix's arm. 'But he seemed really happy with the new keyboard I bought.' She turned to Anna. 'He is – was – a great musician. He does still seem able to play a bit but playing the piano in the lounge disturbs everyone, so I got him one of those little electric things. Now he'll be playing the same thing over and over because he won't remember.'

Anna could see that, behind her unconcerned manner, Cassandra hid real sadness. And she was obviously very caring and generous. She couldn't work out why Felix was so hard on her. She was relieved when Felix went off to change and directed Anna and his mother to the hall where there was to be a talk by his commanding officer. They were about to sit down when Cassandra suddenly turned to Anna, an anxious expression on her face.

'Sorry about all that back there,' she murmured. 'You probably think like Felix, that I'm self-centred, career-minded . . .'

'No, I . . .'

'And maybe I am,' she went on. It seemed as if the floodgates had opened and, once she'd started, she couldn't stop. She wasn't really addressing Anna; it was as though she was talking to herself.

'But you know what? The point that Felix doesn't seem to get is that I can do far more good pressing the Government for changes, more help for carers, wider availability of drugs to deal with this awful disease, than I ever could keeping myself shut away at home trying – and failing – to look after my husband.' She smiled ruefully. 'I'm a very determined woman, and when I believe in something, I'll stop at nothing to bring it to the notice of as many people as I can . . .'

'Yes, I know,' Anna smiled. 'My dad was really keen to get you on the show after that time when you threw all that underwear out of —'

'Oh my God.' Cassandra stared at Anna. 'Anna Eliot,' she said. 'Walter Eliot's your father, isn't he?'

Anna nodded. 'He'd really love to get you on his programme – I mean, what you've just said, it's right. It's so important and if the major parties aren't doing enough to change things, then the public should realise that it's time to vote for the individual, not the party.'

'You're clearly smart,' Cassandra commented. 'I'll think about it. Although, as I told the producer at the time, I prefer to walk the . . .'

'Walk rather than talk the talk,' Anna finished. 'But sometimes you have to talk so that other people get fired up to walk the walk, right?'

Cassandra eyed her thoughtfully. 'I like that,' she said. 'I like it very much. Talk to get others to walk – I might use that.' She nodded. 'You might mention our chat to your father, and I'll get on to it my end. Oh look, here comes Felix – about time. Now let's hear what these military types have got to say for themselves.'

By the end of the talk, Anna's heart was beating rather too rapidly for comfort. It had been one thing to imagine Felix in a war zone, and quite another to see pictures on the screen of what he would be facing. She was relieved when the meeting drew to a close, and people began drifting off to to lunch.

Cassandra had got up and left her seat quickly, without waiting for them.

'Oh God, now what's she doing?' Felix grabbed Anna's wrist and pointed across the room. Cassandra was striding up to the commanding officer, and her shrill tones could be heard above the babble of the assembled guests.

'Glorifying war, that's what you lot are doing . . . hypocrisy . . . make it sound like a jolly game of soldiers . . .'

The commanding officer grew more red in the face with every second, and several people paused and turned to stare in amazement.

'All your talk about a nuclear capability . . .'

Felix pushed his way through the crowd and strode over to his mother. Anna couldn't catch what he was saying as he seized Cassandra's arm but she noticed the officer nod imperceptibly before turning and walking briskly away.

'It's all propaganda and . . .' Cassandra stopped in mid-sentence and glared at his retreating back.

'Well, that makes a change from the usual routine I must say!' A short, stocky man glanced at Anna as she pushed past him and shoved a notebook into his breast pocket. 'Livened things up a bit, that did.'

'They say there's lunch!' Cassandra beckoned to Anna as if nothing untoward had happened. 'I need the loo – see you in the mess hall in ten minutes?'

She gave a cheery wave, apparently oblivious to the critical glances of the other parents, and headed for the door. Anna scanned the room for Felix, and saw that he had caught up with the officer and was deep in conversation. He was rubbing the back of his neck with his left hand, the way he always did when he was uptight.

'Are you OK?' she asked, several minutes later, when he finally made his way towards her.

'I'll never forgive her, never,' he said, his voice shaking. 'The Commandant was great; he said he didn't hold me responsible.'

'He could hardly do that, could he?' Anna reasoned.

'I'll be a laughing stock with the lads,' he mumbled. 'Thank God she's gone.'

'Actually, she's waiting for us over at the mess hall – they said lunch is ready,' Anna ventured.

'She's what? You mean, she expects us to sit and eat with

her after all she's done? She's got to be kidding.'

Anna followed as Felix strode across to the mess hall. They found Cassandra sitting calmly at a table surveying the menu card.

'Now before you start, I'm sorry,' she said, the moment Felix was within earshot.

'It's a bit late for that,' Felix said. 'Mum, what were you thinking?'

'I know, I know, I should have kept my mouth shut,' Cassandra admitted. 'I just got so angry when that man went on about . . . Oh damn!'

She paused as her mobile phone shrilled from her handbag.

'Mum, they're supposed to be switched off,' Felix hissed.

'Sorry, I'll just take this . . .' She flipped the cover and clamped the phone to her ear.

'What? No! Really? They said that – oh my God!'

As her voice rose to a crescendo, diners at the nearby tables stopped speaking and turned to stare. Impervious to their glares and raised eyebrows, she carried on.

'So tell me, how did the Tories react to that one? Did they now?' She whipped a pad and silver pencil out of her bag and began scribbling. 'Got it! You bet I will! This could be just what I need.'

'Mum, for God's sake,' Felix pleaded, as a man on the neighbouring table muttered audibly about the manners of some people being beyond belief. 'Can't you read the sign?'

Cassandra waved her hand impatiently. 'OK, so let's see . . . I could be with you in . . .' She glanced at her watch. 'Four hours max. OK. *Ciao* – oh, and thanks!' She stuffed her mobile back into her bag and turned to Felix.

'Darling, I'm so sorry,' she began. 'But something's cropped up – I'm going to have to go.'

'That suits me fine. Go and be embarrassing somewhere else.'

'Felix, don't be like that. I've said I'm sorry. I know I was out of order.'

'Mum, just go, OK?' Felix said. 'It's fine. Anna's here. And you know what? She actually wants to be here and, surprise, surprise, she knows how to behave.'

'OK, well, I'll be on my way,' she said, bending forward to give Felix a kiss which he deftly dodged, and then turning to Anna and briefly squeezing her hand. 'Good to have met you,' she continued. 'And I'm sure we'll meet again, one way or another. *Ciao* now!'

Anna was so busy concentrating on Felix that she didn't notice the stocky man from the talk get up from a neighbouring table and hurry after Cassandra. Nor did she notice that slung over his shoulder was a very expensive-looking camera bag.

To Anna's relief, the recruits were allowed the evening off to be with their guests and so she and Felix were able to be by themselves again. It had taken him ages to calm down, but Zac, Phoebe and Mrs Harville, who had witnessed the whole scene in the lecture hall, assured him that everyone would forget it in next to no time. Mrs Harville was very gracious and said it was probably all down to her love for Felix and fear for his well-being.

While the Harvilles went off to Exeter for the evening, Felix and Anna headed into Exmouth, bought fish and chips and sat on the sea wall, eating them out of paper and talking non-stop. At first, all Felix could talk about was his anger at his mother, but when Anna mentioned his mother had said she was keen to campaign for drugs to be made available to everyone suffering from Alzheimer's, he calmed down a bit and grudgingly said that time would tell, and at least if she focused on that she might leave him to get on with his own life and do something, however indirect, to help his dad.

'And now, your surprise,' she said, desperate to change the subject, and handed him the concert tickets. 'It's way ahead, but you said they were your favourite band and I had to act fast – they were all sold out within hours of going online.'

He was totally overwhelmed, and told her that no one had ever meant as much to him as she did. 'The fact that you went to all that trouble and expense just for me – I'm blown away!'

And then the talking stopped and they had walked down to the water's edge, and, ignoring the rapidly falling temperature, kissed and sank down on to the sand and gazed up at the darkening sky and tried not to think about all the weeks that would have to pass before they could be together again. He walked with her to the station and waved the train off, and suddenly Anna realised why everyone cried at *Brief Encounter*. She tried to remain upbeat because Mrs Harville looked weepy and Phoebe was far quieter than usual, but when she finally got home and closed her bedroom door, and flicked the pages of her diary to count how many days would have to pass before she saw Felix again, she couldn't hold the tears back any longer.

✖ CHAPTER 8 ✖

*'One man's ways may be as good as another's
but we all like our own best.'*
(Jane Austen, *Persuasion*)

'ANNA? IN HERE! NOW!'

Anna had been about to leave for school the following
Monday morning when her father flung open his study
door and called to her.

'You're in the paper!' he cried, thrusting it under her
nose. 'Not that it's a particularly flattering picture.'

Anna dropped her bag on to the floor and seized the
paper. Her father had folded it back to the In The Know
diary section where a picture of Cassandra, arms waving,
and Felix looking moody and scowling, took the centre of
the page. And at the edge of the picture was Anna, a
nervous expression on her face, her tongue protruding
slightly the way it always did when she was anxious.

*UNDER FIRE – PROSPECTIVE MP HURLS A
BROADSIDE AT THE MARINES*

Anna's eyes scanned the page.

*Cassandra Wentworth, who is standing as an Independent
in the forthcoming Muckleborough and Bythorn by-election,*

has never made a secret of her pacifist viewpoint. A regular at the Greenham Common Women's Peace Camp in the early eighties and one of the motivating forces behind countless protests about research laboratories across the country, she has more recently been at the forefront of many peace campaigns. Clearly the decision by her son, Felix, to join the Royal Marines does not sit well with her. At an Open Day for families of new recruits, held at the Commando Training Centre in Lympstone on Saturday, she was extremely vocal about her views on the military . . .

'You didn't mention any of this,' her father challenged her. 'I mean, this is powerful stuff.'

Anna frowned as she read the next paragraph.

I asked her how she felt when her nineteen-year-old son announced his intention of joining the Marines.

'Felix is his own man,' she said. 'He may not share my moral values, and I'm certainly not comfortable seeing all this show of force, but I'm his mum first and foremost. It pains me to see what he is doing, but all I can hope is that he will see sense and realise that he could spend his time so much more profitably.'

'It's this bit that matters,' her father said, prodding a paragraph that he had already marked with a yellow highlighter pen.

Ms Wentworth, who is standing as an Independent in protest at what she calls 'the inefficacy of party politics', went on to say that his girlfriend, Anna Eliot (pictured above left with Ms Wentworth and son Felix), the daughter of the well-known television personality and host of Walt on Wednesday *and* Walt at the Weekend, *shared her views and was equally distressed by her son's decision and wished he had chosen a different career path.*

'I didn't say that,' Anna muttered.

'Wonderful plug for the show there,' Walter enthused, ignoring her completely. 'And for me, of course.' He pointed at the small inset head and shoulders picture of himself to the left of the text.

'We must get her on the show as soon as possible. Could make for great viewing.' He smiled at Anna. 'Much as I don't approve of you hanging out with this Felix guy, at least something good has come out of it, and it's not as if it'll go anywhere.'

'What do you mean?'

'Anna, be sensible. Working-class black guy and a mother who is clearly totally off the wall . . . No common ground between you at all. And as for the mother . . .'

'Actually, she's rather nice. And I feel quite sorry for her.'

'Why?'

'She's having a tough time, what with her husband in a home and . . .'

'A home? Go on.'

By the time she had filled her father in on the details, she was relieved to see his attitude had changed from one of eager anticipation of controversy to a concerned and compassionate desire to allow Cassandra air time to push for changes to government policy. Within minutes, he was on the phone deep in conversation with his producer.

'Now that,' she heard him say as she collected her things and headed for the door, 'is something worth pursuing. Alzheimer's . . . yes, exactly! Get the researchers on to it!'

Good, she thought. *He'll be gentle on her, Felix will see that she really is concerned about his dad and raising Alzheimer's awareness, and Dad'll realise that Felix isn't as bad as he thinks.*

It was to be only a few days before she realised that where her father was concerned, it was foolish to make such assumptions.

'So come on, dish the dirt – what happened exactly? I want every last detail.' Shannon grabbed Anna's arm as she arrived in the Sixth Form common room on Monday.

'Oh no,' Anna groaned. 'Who else knows?'

'Knows what?' Shannon frowned. 'That Saturday was the big lurve-in? Mia, Lauren, and anyone else within earshot of you all last week!'

'So you didn't see the paper?'

Shannon frowned. 'What paper?'

'Never mind,' Anna said hastily, as out of the corner of her eye she spotted Mia and Lauren heading her way.

'So how was it with the love of your life?' Lauren asked. 'Did you have a big romantic farewell?'

'Don't get her started,' Mia chipped in. 'We've got more important things to sort right now – like the music for the band.'

Anna felt a surge of relief. If anything could take her mind off Felix, it was music. Wild Chicks had been her brainwave during her first term at Fleckford College, and it had cemented the new friendship between her, Shannon, Mia who played drums, and Lauren – the best double bass player Anna had ever heard. They were doing well; Mr Longhurst, the head of music, had encouraged them to enter the Fleckford Music Festival, and when they won second place in their class playing Anna and Shannon's new composition, 'Rattlesnake Stomp', he had told them that he was throwing a party for his parents' Golden Wedding in June and, if by then they were up to scratch, they could play in the hallway of his house as a surprise to greet his mum and dad on their arrival.

'My father's a jazz fanatic,' he had told them. 'Chicago style, Bebop, fusion – you name it, he goes wild for it.'

The concept of anyone old enough to be the grey-haired Mr Longhurst's father going wild had reduced Lauren to a fit of the giggles but, when he had offered them hard cash if they would agree to play, they had become seriously enthusiastic.

'Mia's right. If we mess up we don't get paid,' Anna reminded them now. 'How about we meet up after school every day this week and give it all we've got?'

'Every day?' Lauren groaned.

Anna smiled. She knew that concentrating on playing was the only thing that would keep her mind off Felix and the seemingly interminable weeks she had to wait before seeing him again.

Thanks to Araminta's persistence and Cassandra's desire for publicity, Walter managed to get her on the programme the following Saturday. Marina poured two glasses of wine and handed one to Anna. 'This will be good,' she said enthusiastically. 'Your father is such a skilled interviewer.'

'You hit the headlines in a rather spectacular manner this week,' Walter began, his legs crossed as he smiled amiably in what Anna knew was an attempt to lull his guest into a

false sense of security. '*Your views on the military are well known . . . you are anti-war, am I right?*'

'*I am against violence and conflict of all sorts,*' she said.

Walter nodded sagely and suddenly switched topics and asked her to talk about her campaign for more help for carers and easier access to drugs that could treat Alzheimer's. Cassandra grew more and more enthusiastic, speaking energetically about her distress over her husband's decline and looking directly at the camera. She spoke of the need for far more research into the illness, and insisted that the Government should do all in its power to increase the funds available. The studio audience were clearly rooting for her, and her remarks were peppered by bursts of applause.

And that was when Walter's tone changed.

'*For the sake of our no doubt bemused viewers, let me get this perfectly straight. You are against violence and conflict —*'

'*I am against violence and conflict of any sort . . . Yes.*'

'*And yet you have in the past been prepared to use physical violence in an attempt to prevent research work of which you are now suddenly in favour? Correct me if I'm wrong.*'

Cassandra's mouth dropped open and for a moment she was speechless.

'*Let me put it simply for you,*' Walter went on, adopting the tone of one speaking to a rather confused and distracted child. '*Not long ago, you were at the forefront of the protests on animal testing – indeed you appeared in court having vandalised a laboratory, I believe?*'

There was an audible gasp from the studio audience.

'*I fail to see the relevance . . .*' Cassandra stammered.

'*The laboratories which you and your fellow protestors*'

targeted four years ago, are the very ones that were testing the drug you now say must be made available to everyone. A strange change of heart, is it not?'

'Tee hee,' Marina chuckled. 'I do love high definition TV – it shows off their blushes so well!'

'Join us after the break . . .' Walter smiled to the camera. *'. . . when I will be asking Ms Wentworth to share with us any elements in her manifesto that do actually hold water.'*

Anna picked up the remote control and zapped the sound while the adverts were on. She was used to the way her father pulled his studio guests to pieces and had always thought it rather clever, in a sadistic sort of way. This time she wanted to wring his neck.

Anna forced her eyes open as the house phone rang persistently. Groping for her bedside clock, she peered at the dial.

Six-thirty a.m. Felix! It could only be Felix. She leaped out of bed, sped down the stairs and grabbed the handset, thinking that she must have forgotten to charge her mobile.

'Hello?'

'May I speak to Walter Eliot please?' a woman's voice with a slight Scottish burr demanded.

Anna's heart sank like a stone. 'He's asleep,' she said. 'He did a show last night and . . .'

'I'm only too well aware of that,' said the voice at the other end. 'That's the reason I'm ringing. It's Valerie, the show's producer. It's urgent, so please will you get him?'

'He won't like it,' Anna ventured to suggest.

'Too flaming right he won't,' Valerie snapped. 'But he'll

like it even less if he doesn't speak to me at once while I have the chance to save his skin.'

'This is preposterous! It's outrageous – how dare she . . .? And to summon me to the studios as if I were some minion to be ordered about . . .'

The air in the kitchen was blue with expletives when, twenty minutes later, Anna came down to breakfast. Marina, who had spent the night at the house having decided that driving home after a large glass of wine was hardly sensible, was leaning against the breakfast bar, sipping coffee and looking none too pleased at being woken before eight-thirty.

'What's wrong?' Anna asked.

'What's wrong? Someone – well, clearly it's that wretched Wentworth woman – has lodged some pathetic little complaint about me,' Walter blustered. 'Valerie says it's too sensitive to go into details on the telephone. What a load of utter rubbish!'

'Dad, calm down, it's probably nothing major,' Anna said. 'People have complained before and you've sorted it.'

'And sorting Ms Wentworth will give me the greatest pleasure,' her father declared. 'I knew the moment I saw her that she was trouble. Well, she'll soon learn that you don't mess with Walter Eliot.'

❧ CHAPTER 9 ❧

'Vanity was the beginning
and end of . . . Walter Eliot's character.'
(Jane Austen, *Persuasion*)

'HI, IT'S SHANNON! I SAW THE PROGRAMME LAST NIGHT –
oh my God!'

'You don't know the half of it,' Anna sighed. 'All hell's
been let loose since then. Apparently . . . hang on a
minute!'

She paused as the front door slammed. Within seconds,
the kitchen door flew open. Her father stood in the
doorway. His face was as white as a sheet.

'Sorry – Dad's back – got to go,' Anna muttered down
the phone. 'I'll call you in a bit.'

She tossed the phone to one side as her father slumped
down in the nearest chair and rested his head in his hands.

'Dad? Dad, are you OK?' Anna asked.

'No.' His voice was thick with emotion. 'In fact, I'm far
from OK.'

Every fibre of Anna's being went on red alert. She knew
her father so well – and normally, if something or someone
had upset him, he would have been swearing and

slamming doors and shouting the house down. Instead, he looked drained and diminshed.

'Are you ill?' she gasped, memories of the day her mum admitted how ill she was flooding back into her mind.

'No, I'm not ill,' he said quietly. 'I've been accused of something. Wrongly accused – I didn't do it. I swear to you on your darling mother's memory, I didn't do it.'

From that moment on, the day became a bit of a blur. Walter, silent and morose, refusing food but drinking whisky in a rather alarming manner, Araminta turning up a couple of hours later (much to Marina's annoyance) and Anna being told to field phone calls, most of which were from the press.

'OK, now let's get this perfectly clear,' Araminta said, removing the bottle of Glenmorangie and sitting down beside Walter on the white leather sofa. 'You were in the Green Room after the show talking to Valerie, the producer, and your other guest, Jack what'shisname from that new soap, right?

'Jack Flanders,' he nodded.

'And Cassandra was there?' Araminta took his hand, while Marina looked on daggers drawn.

'Briefly – said she was going on to some reception.'

'Anyone else?'

'Of course someone else,' Walter snapped, the alcohol bringing back patches of florid colour to his cheeks. 'The place was teeming – put a tray of free canapés on a table and they descend like flaming locusts!'

'According to Valerie, Cassandra is adamant that, not only did you humiliate her on air,' Araminta pressed on, 'but that Jack swore to her that you made blatantly racist comments about Anna hanging out with some ill-educated half-caste – his words, not mine!'

'Dad, you didn't . . .' Anna gasped.

'Of course I didn't!' Walter returned. 'I may not approve of you two going out but I'm not a total idiot. Would I honestly jeopardise my career, which isn't exactly thriving right now, by uttering such obscenities?'

Anna realised things must be bad. Her father would never normally admit that he was anything but a number one star.

'But am I right in thinking there was something else?' Marina ventured. 'Some ridiculous suggestion that you actually said that if you were Cassandra's husband you'd choose to go mad rather than have to live with her?'

Walter fiddled nervously with his bow tie. 'I – well, I mean obviously that was a joke – and clearly not meant for anyone's ears except Valerie's. Not my fault Jack flaming Flanders was earwigging in on the conversation.'

He glanced round at their frozen expressions.

'Oh come on, people say things like that all the time at dinner parties,' he reasoned. 'I didn't mean anything by it.'

'What you did or did not mean is hardly the point right now,' Araminta sighed. 'We can probably paper over that one – but the remark about Felix . . .' She looked at Walter, a stern expression on her face. 'You swear you didn't say anything racist about him?'

'No, truly – I mean, the only thing . . .'

'Go on.'

'The only thing someone might have heard,' he continued, glancing nervously at Anna, 'was when I said to Val that I hoped there was some truth in the saying "out of sight, out of mind" because the sooner . . .'

'Yes?'

'The sooner Anna started mixing with her own kind the better.'

'Dad, I just don't believe you!' Anna exploded, half out of anger at his prejudice and half out of fear that Felix would somehow blame her. 'You know what? You are unbelievable!'

'I'm sorry, darling.'

'It's too late for sorry, I fear,' Marina cut in. 'We'll just have to hope and pray that some big news breaks overnight. Otherwise the press could run with this big time.'

For days after that disastrous show, Walter was a man in shock. His time was spent on the phone, in meetings with Araminta and the TV company and glued to his laptop, monitoring the public's response to the outcry that followed the programme and the Green Room report. From time to time, he would shout 'Precisely!' when someone said that, since the remarks, if they had been made at all, had been made off air, the producers were making a mountain out of a molehill; but more often, he would sit, head in hands, muttering expletives at those who wrote that such comments should never be thought, never mind uttered, and that Eliot was clearly a mindless buffoon who should be sacked immediately.

'How many more times do I have to tell them? I didn't say all that,' he would say to no one in particular.

Anna felt as if she was living in the middle of a war

zone. Her father sought solace in the whisky bottle, which made him alternately overconfident and then deeply morose; her mates at school, with the exception of Shannon, kept asking questions and clearly relished all the gossip and comments in the tabloid press; Mallory rang from Swancote Hall every evening saying she was suffering from stress and Gabriella stormed home at the weekend, accusing Anna of being the cause of all the trouble for associating with Felix in the first place.

'I tried to tell her, Dad,' she said in the honeyed tones she always used when maximising her position as Walter's favourite. 'I said that family were trouble but she wouldn't listen.'

'I feel like Hamlet, more sinned against than sinning,' Walter said, pulling open a drawer and taking out his binoculars.

'King Lear,' Anna muttered.

'What?'

'Lear, not Hamlet,' she told him. 'Where are you going?'

'Kempton Park,' he replied. 'Surely you remember? Hampton Heroine's running in the four-thirty. Gaby's coming. Do you want to join us?'

Anna shook her head. 'No, the band's playing at that party I told you about,' she said. 'And I've loads to do first.' The most important of which was emailing Felix.

She had sent him a message straight after the show.

To: fxw@talktalk.net
From: saxygirl@tiscali.net
Hi! I'm sorry – I didn't know things would turn out like that. The programme, I mean? You did see it, didn't you? Parents –

what a liability! It won't make any difference to us, though, will it? Love you loads, Anna xxx

His reply had reassured her.

To: *saxygirl@tiscali.net*
From: *fxw@talktalk.net*
Didn't see the show but one of the guys here said my mum came over as really cool! Got to dash but will call later, OK? Miss you loads. F x

The following day, after all the papers had seen fit to splash the news of Walter's faux pas all over the front pages, he emailed again.

To: *saxygirl@tiscali.net*
From: *fxw@talktalk.net*
Mum has emailed me. Surprised words weren't purple. She's outraged about your dad's remarks – I don't know who he thinks he is thinking he can get away with using language like that. Parents! F x

Anna had emailed back at once, telling Felix that her dad swore he didn't say those things and avoiding any mention of what he did say. She said how much she loved him and how nothing but that mattered.

To: *saxygirl@tiscali.net*
From: *fxw@ talktalk.net*
Everything mad here. Will be in touch when I can. F

'So what does that mean?' Anna demanded of Shannon as they prepared for the party at Mr Longhurst's house. 'There's no kiss at the end. And what does "when I can" mean? Do you think he's going to dump me just because of my dad?'

'You read too much into things,' Shannon replied. 'I mean, he probably had a load of mates peering over his shoulder – you know what boys are like, they can't bear to be seen as soppy.'

'You really think that was it?'

'Sure to be,' Shannon replied airily. 'Have you seen the buffet? I'm so glad I said we needed refreshments if we were going to play. There's a chocolate pudding to die for.'

Despite Araminta's constant reassurances to Walter that the whole thing would blow over, it didn't. Walter was suspended from any further shows and then, in mid July, he was told that his contract would not be renewed.

For a couple of weeks, Walter was moody, depressed and angry by turns. Then, after putting the whole matter into the hands of some very expensive and highly regarded lawyers, he set about entertaining all his friends and acquaintances in an even more lavish manner than before. Not only did he invite ten friends to a house he had rented on the Isle of Wight for Cowes Week, he booked boxes at several race meetings and gambled heavily on every horse that took his fancy. He also threw several dinner parties with food from London caterers and enormous quantities of vintage champagne. And at all these events, to Marina's annoyance and Anna's alarm, Araminta was more than happy to play the role of hostess.

'Walter, don't you think you should rein in a bit?' Marina asked him on more than one occasion. 'You don't know what the future holds and, if you carry on at this rate, you'll run out of cash.'

'I've plenty of irons in the fire,' he assured her. 'You wait – I'll have a dozen channels clamouring for me by September. Let me enjoy my free time while I can.'

He certainly seemed more relaxed and Anna was too excited at the thought of Felix's return home to think of much else. She assumed that the lawyers were doing their stuff and that everything would be sorted.

That might have happened, had it not been for the fickle public and the result of the Muckleborough and Bythorn by-election. Cassandra Wentworth got in with a majority of 242, which, while not by any means a comfortable majority, was so unexpected that it hit the headlines in all the major national newspapers, many of which reminded its readers of what more and more were calling 'The Walter-gate affair'.

And then Felix came up with his great idea.

❧ CHAPTER 10 ❧

'What wild imaginations one forms
where dear self is involved.'
(Jane Austen, *Persuasion*)

'WHAT ARE YOU DOING THE SECOND WEEK IN AUGUST?'

The phone call from Felix came through on Anna's mobile on the next to last day of the summer term, just minutes before the band were due to play in their slot at the Summer Spectacular, the concert in which the college showcased its achievements for the year.

'Nothing special. Why?'

'Anna!' Lauren hissed, nudging her elbow. 'Get off the phone – we're due on in five minutes.'

Anna waved her away, straining to hear Felix above the chatter of her classmates.

'Zac's grandmother has got this house on the Isle of Wight, right? She's going off to Australia to see her sister, and has said that Zac and Phoebe can use it,' he told her. 'Phoebe's taking Jamie, Zac's got this new girlfriend, Ursula, and well – he suggested you and I go too. What do you say?'

Anna's heart raced. A whole week away with Felix;

there was only one answer. An image of Marina and her father scowling angrily flashed through her mind but she banished them and took a deep breath.

'That would be amazing!' she replied. 'Look, it's our school end of year bash – I've got to go but . . .'

'We need time together,' Felix said. 'But there is just one more thing. We'd have to go a day later than the others, because the day after I get back Mum wants us both to join her. The thing is, it's . . .'

'Anna!' Shannon poked her in the ribs. 'Come on!'

'Sssh – I'll be there in a minute!' Anna mouthed back.

' . . . so you see, it's really important. Don't you agree?'

Since Anna hadn't a clue what he'd just said, she hesitated for a second. The thought of spending time with Cassandra wasn't something that filled her with unmitigated joy, but if Felix said it was important . . .

'Or is that going to be a bridge too far? I mean don't bother if your dad . . .' Felix began.

'No, no – of course, it'll be great. Can't wait. Fill me in on the details later, OK? Got to dash. Love you loads.'

She blew a kiss down the phone and then pulled a face at Shannon and Mia, who were rolling their eyes and pretending to swoon.

'I take it,' Shannon smiled as Anna switched her phone to silent and stuffed it into her bag, 'that the love life is progressing nicely?'

'Dreamily!' sighed Anna. 'It doesn't get any better than this. I feel like I've died and gone to heaven.'

As with most highs, the low came a few hours later. As her father blustered and bluffed his way around the college displays, chest puffed out when someone recognised him and cheeks suffused with colour when the odd person dared to question him about the headlines that were clearly still in people's minds, the question loomed large in Anna's mind. Just how was she going to approach the subject of staying away a week with Felix? She had avoided all mention of his name, just as her dad had done; it was as if there was an unwritten rule in the house that what Marina called 'that nasty business' was never to be spoken of again.

'I don't know how to tell him without him being furious,' Anna explained to Shannon later that afternoon on the way to the traditional end of term raid on the cake shop.

'By not mentioning Felix, silly,' Shannon replied. 'What he doesn't know can't hurt him.'

'So – just say I'm going on holiday with Zac and Phoebe, you mean?'

'Why not? It's not like you're lying – just being selective with the truth.'

'I guess you're right – and if he does find out that Felix is there too, well – Zac's free to invite who he likes, right?'

'Precisely!' Shannon said. 'At last you appear to be getting the hang of dealing with parents. About time too, if you don't mind me saying so!'

Anna, adamant about not telling the full story about the forthcoming holiday, had also decided not to mention Felix's homecoming to any of her family; they hadn't realised that he would have leave from training in the summer and she was very happy to keep it that way.

Luckily for Anna, her father was so preoccupied with his own affairs that, when she finally mentioned to him that she was going to the Isle of Wight with Phoebe and a crowd of her mates (mentioning Zac would have only brought Felix to mind), he merely grunted and said he couldn't see the attraction of the place unless you could go in Cowes Week, which she wasn't.

'Anyway, you go and have a good time – I shall be rushed off my feet all week,' he went on. 'Araminta's lined up a whole raft of meetings for me – she's sure she can land me the sort of slot that my talents deserve, and then, of course, I've the magazine interviews to do.' (Walter had been in demand with several celebrity glossies that ran features with headlines such as: *My Fight to Clear My Name* and *Walter's Wednesday's Full of Woe*. Far from avoiding drawing attention to the issue, he revelled in playing the role of misunderstood victim.)

'The Isle of Wight? What do you want to go there for? It's so nineteen-fifties,' sneered Gabriella, who had arrived back from college high on the news that her new boyfriend's parents had asked her to join them for two weeks at their timeshare in Tenerife. 'Me, I know how to have a good time – after Tenerife, Sophie and I are going to Paris for Shelby's hen weekend and then meeting up with a whole crowd at this house in Burgundy.'

'That'll cost a bomb,' Anna ventured. 'I don't think Dad can afford to keep subbing us.'

'It's peanuts on Eurostar,' Gaby replied. 'And I have a way of getting other people to pay for me.' She made it sound like a gifted accomplishment, but Anna was too glad that she wasn't going to be hanging around to bother arguing.

{131}

'So Gaby'll be away, you'll be on the Isle of Wight, and I'll be stuck here all on my own, with just Marina hanging about – it's not fair,' moaned Mallory.

'Don't be silly,' Anna protested. 'Henrietta and Lou will be around. You can hang out with them.'

'They're going all funny with me,' Mallory grumbled. 'The other day they were teasing me like anything – even Charlie told them to lay off me. He's really nice to me – he's invited me to the Young Farmers' Ball.'

'Charlie invited you?' The summer ball was another must-do in the Eliot–Musgrove social calendar and this would be the first time that Mallory had gone with a partner.

'Well, don't sound so surprised,' Mallory retorted. 'Just because you'll be there without a guy, that's not my problem. Oh, and can I borrow your gold sandals?'

Anna lay awake for hours the night before Felix was due home, just dreaming about how it would be when she saw him. They had arranged to meet on the Friday evening at the same spot in Kellynch Woods where they had said goodbye back in April, and she pictured herself, wearing her new black and white mini dress and scarlet pumps, running lightly down the path and into his arms. There was then a slow motion sequence, during which their lips met and they sank to their knees in ecstatic embrace.

In the event, she saw him before he saw her, rushed down the path and fell over a tree root, sending her bag flying and gashing her knee on a broken branch. The dreamed-of moments of tender embrace and lingering kisses were spent dusting twigs out of her hair and mopping her bleeding knee with the sleeve of his shirt. The romance was further killed by the fact that he couldn't stop laughing.

'I'm sorry,' he gasped. 'But you looked so funny – and adorable!'

'Just focus on the adorable, will you?' she pleaded, clenching her teeth against the throbbing of her knee. For a moment, she felt almost shy with him – he seemed somehow to have changed. He stood taller, and had a new air of confidence about him.

'Come here,' he murmured. He wrapped his arms around her and she breathed in the distinctive smell of him, her eyes filling with tears.

'Does it hurt that badly?' he asked.

'It's not that,' she whispered. 'It's just that I've missed you so much and Dad's lost his job and he's drinking like crazy.'

'But you're here, and that's what matters,' Felix said. 'Mum's been really decent about it all, actually – considering what your dad said and everything.'

Anna opened her mouth to protest that her father's only admission was the fact that maybe he had been a bit forceful on camera.

'Shhh,' Felix said. 'Enough talking.'

And he kissed her. And it was so good that she decided it wasn't really worth making an issue about parents after all.

Later, sitting outside the Anchor Inn, sipping lime sodas, Felix told her everything about the holiday home, the travel plans and all the things he thought she might like to do there.

'But right now, we need to sort tomorrow out,' he said. 'You are still up for it?'

'Up for what?' Anna frowned.

'I told you on the phone – the big lunch thing with Mum,' he said. 'You know, maybe I've been a bit hard on her. Despite everything, she's really keen for you to be at this lunch.'

'Lunch?' Anna queried. 'Oh, I thought . . .'

'I told you,' Felix replied, a touch impatiently. 'It's the Memory Munch Lunch – in aid of Alzheimer's. They do them all over the country and Mum's on the organising committee for this one – and she wants us there. Well, helping with the serving to start with but we get to eat as well!'

'You're sure she's up for me going? I mean, we didn't exactly get off to a good start.'

'That's the whole point,' Felix said. 'She said she didn't want all this business between her and your dad to mess up our relationship.'

He took a long swig of his drink and reached for her hand. 'And you know what? I think Mum and I are getting on better – we've had some massive rows over the past few weeks, and exchanged some pretty heated emails but I think I get where she's coming from now. She'll always say exactly what she thinks and she's never going to approve of my career – but she's agreed to drop that subject once and for all. And at least she's doing more stuff for Dad and not prancing about shoving herself into the limelight.'

It did occur to Anna that since Parliament was on summer recess, there wasn't much opportunity for Cassandra to show off, but she refrained from saying so. She was just relieved that everything was back on solid ground once more.

All she had to do now was enjoy spending time with Felix.

'I'm so glad you could come!' Cassandra, elegant in white linen trousers and a lime-green silk shirt, kissed Anna on both cheeks. 'And before you say a word, can we wipe the slate clean and start afresh? It's not your fault your father is a racist idiot and —'

'Mum!' Felix shot her a warning glance.

'The thing that matters is that you matter to Felix and he matters to me. Friends?' She looked at Anna pleadingly.

'Absolutely,' Anna smiled.

'Wonderful!' Cassandra said, clapping her hands. 'And now if you two could just hand round the trays of canapés, while I do the meet-and-greet bit, that would be splendid.'

Anna, to her surprise, enjoyed every minute of the event. It wasn't the stuffy occasion full of well-heeled county types that she had expected; there were lots of young families milling around the gardens, enjoying face painting, kite making and a Punch and Judy show; there was croquet on the lawn, plant stalls in the orchard and a tombola on the verandah. Lunch was buffet style served on trestle tables covered with gingham cloths, to the accompaniment of a string quartet which, Anna noted with a degree of satisfaction, was not nearly as good as Wild Chicks even though the members were more than twice their age.

'People are spending money like it grows on trees,' Cassandra whispered in Anna's ear at the end of lunch, 'and you know what? Felix is doing a wonderful job – he even spoke to the reporter from *South Today* about his dad and what it feels like to see someone you love slowly disintegrating – oh my dear! I'm sorry, how tactless of me! Felix told me about your mother . . .'

'It's OK,' Anna assured her, astonished at the change in a woman she had made up her mind to hate. 'I'm glad he's talking about it. And if it gets on the local news, that would be awesome.'

'I know, but I guess they'll edit it right down and just show a ten-second clip,' Cassandra laughed. 'Right, now for the big finale – the balloon race!

Everyone, Anna included, had bought a biodegradable balloon for five pounds, and the one that flew the furthest would win.

'Over here, everyone!' Cassandra shouted through a megaphone as one of her committee staggered up with huge bunches of multi-coloured balloons. 'Thank you all so much.'

'Let's hope she doesn't go on too much,' Felix whispered, sidling up to Anna and putting his arm around her shoulder. 'She's kept a remarkably low profile for her so far.'

'And now perhaps the children would like to gather round while I invite Anna Eliot and my son, Felix, to cut the cords that will release the balloons.'

She turned to Anna and proferred a giant pair of bright red scissors as clusters of small kids ran up to her.

'Me? But . . .'

'Go on,' Felix urged, shoving her forward. 'Just let's do it – then we can leave and be on our own.'

Anna and Felix squatted down to the level of the

children and sliced through the cords on every bunch. The children cheered and Anna, shielding her eyes from the glare of the afternoon sun, couldn't help laughing out loud as she watched the balloons soar upwards. As she clambered to her feet, Cassandra gave her a hug and kissed her on both cheeks.

'Thank you so much for being here,' she said yet again. 'It's meant more to me than I can say.'

'Me too,' Anna smiled. And she meant it.

❧ CHAPTER 11 ❧

'All I claim for my own sex . . .
is that of loving longest when hope is gone.'
(Jane Austen, *Persuasion*)

'THIS IS SO PERFECT!' ANNA STOOD ON THE FRONT STEPS of the cottage early on Monday morning, gazing over open farmland towards the sea which was shimmering under a heat haze. Way above her she could hear the song of skylarks, something she hadn't heard in years in Buckinghamshire; behind her, St Catherine's Down was dotted with grazing sheep. They had arrived on the Isle of Wight the previous day and already to Anna it felt as if she was a million miles from all the problems and pressures of home.

'And we've got the rest of the week to do whatever we want,' Felix said, coming up behind her, wrapping his arms around her and nibbling her right ear. 'What do you say we head for the beach?'

'What about the others?'

'Jamie and Phoebe are in the middle of a row, and Zac and Sula were last seen disappearing up the hill hand in hand and lip to lip!'

The moment they had met the previous afternoon, Anna couldn't help noticing how Ursula looked so like Gaby that she could have been her twin. The same dark eyes and ivory skin, the same long mane of shiny hair. But there was a difference; Sula, as all her friends called her, was quieter and clearly adored Zac, always telling him how wonderful he was. Zac, in turn, was as besotted with Sula as he had been with Gaby.

Three hours later, lying on the sand at Compton Bay, almost purring as Felix languidly rubbed sun lotion on to her back, Anna felt as if she could die from pure happiness. Several girls on the beach had eyed Felix up earlier as he ran down the beach and into the sea, diving under the breaking surf and surfacing, blowing her a kiss with the light shimmering off his dark body. She could almost feel their envy as she ran towards him and let him whirl her round and dunk her under the water; and she felt a sense of total freedom and release.

'I wish this could go on for ever,' she sighed, rolling on to her back and running her hands through her long damp hair. 'I don't want anything to change.'

'But it will,' Felix said. 'And I worry that . . .' He paused, picking up a shell and turning it over and over in his hands.

'Worry about what?'

'What will happen when my training's over and we get deployed somewhere. What if I get sent abroad? How will you be then?'

'If you mean will I give up on us, you know the answer.'

'I know – it's just – well, I'm not stupid. You've got to have a life and with me miles away, and you off to uni next year, meeting loads of boys that it'll be easier for you to be with . . .'

'Come on! No one's easier to be with than you . . .'

'You know what I mean. Boys actually in the same place as you, from the same background, boys your family would approve of.'

'I just want you, no one else,' Anna said. 'I don't care what my family think. So could you get that into your head once and for all?'

'I . . .'

She pushed him back on the sand and pressed her lips against his. And for a long while, neither of them said another word.

It was later that evening when everything went horribly wrong. The six of them were in the tiny garden of the cottage, lounging about, replete after a barbecue and rather a lot of Pimm's. Jamie and Phoebe were speaking to one another again, albeit in monosyllables, and Sula was strumming her guitar while Zac gazed at her adoringly. Anna had just stirred the fading embers of the barbecue back to life and threaded some marshmallows on to a skewer when the landline in the cottage shrilled loudly.

'Someone get that,' Zac yawned. 'I can't move I'm so full.'

'Your last servant died of overwork, did he?' Felix teased, getting to his feet. 'I'll go.'

In the weeks to come, Anna would close her eyes and hold that moment in her memory as the last in which she was truly happy. At the time, all she was bothered about was not scorching the marshmallows.

'Hello?' She could just catch Felix's voice above the guitar music. 'No – it's Felix. Felix Wentworth. What do you mean, what am I doing here?'

Anna froze, skewer in hand and her heart in her mouth.

'I'll call her.' The sound of the handset crashing on to the table was followed by Felix, storming through the French windows, face like thunder.

'For you. Your father.' He glared at her. 'Who clearly wasn't told just who his precious daughter was with!'

Five pairs of eyes were fixed on Anna as she went into the house and picked up the phone. Walking through to the kitchen in order to be out of earshot, she took a deep breath.

'Hi, Dad. What's up?'

'Well, you've really done it, haven't you? Hit rock bottom in the loyalty stakes. And as if that wasn't enough – you lie to me, go behind my back . . .'

The tirade that assailed her ears was ferocious, even by her father's standards. He carried on in much the same vein before finally running out of breath.

'Well, what have you got to say for yourself?' he demanded.

'I – I don't know what you mean,' she stammered.

'Really? Well, let me help you,' her father replied sarcastically. 'I switch the TV on and there you are, on *South Today*, beaming up at that – that poisonous Cassandra Wentworth as if she were your fairy godmother, not the woman who has just wrecked your father's career. And then kissing the bloody woman as if she was your favourite aunt! How could you? How dare you!'

{141}

'It was just a charity thing,' Anna reasoned, shocked at her father's words. 'For Alzheimer's.'

'Anna, do you have the first idea what you've done? I'm in the middle of a legal battle, and there you are on television, sucking up to the woman who slandered my good name. Hardly gives credence to my case, does it?'

'I didn't think . . .'

'No, clearly you didn't!' her father stormed. 'You've made me look a fool – I can just see the headlines now. It makes me feel sick just thinking about it.'

'Dad, you're overreacting.'

'And now as if that wasn't enough, I find that you've sneaked off behind my back on some sleazy little trip with the son of . . .'

'I didn't sneak off and it isn't sleazy!' Anna shouted. 'I told you about it, and you told me to go and have a good time.'

'You said Phoebe had invited you,' her father replied furiously. 'You made it sound like some girly holiday. And you think you can go behind my back, keeping your phone switched off . . .'

'It's not off, it's just that there's no signal in the cottage . . .'

'And so I telephone Phoebe's mother and discover that – that boy is with you! And there was me thinking he was safely out of the way in Devon.'

'I'm sorry but . . .'

'A bit late for sorry, isn't it?' her father ranted. 'There's just one thing I'm pleased about.'

'What?' Anna asked hopefully.

'That your poor mother isn't around to see what you're doing,' he said.

'Dad, don't say that!'

'I want you home, Anna. Now!'

'No way, Dad,' Anna replied, struggling to keep the tears at bay. 'We've only just got here and we've got plans.'

'So let's see what's more important to you – your precious plans or family loyalty.'

'But Dad . . .'

It was too late for any further protests. Her father had hung up.

'So you lied.'

Felix had sat through Anna's account of the phone call in stony silence and now he was looking at her in disbelief. The others had slipped away, clearly anxious to put space between themselves and Felix's tight-lipped anger.

'I didn't lie,' Anna protested. 'I just didn't tell him the whole truth.'

'I'm not talking about what you did or didn't say to your father,' he snapped. 'I'm talking about the lies you told me.'

'I've never lied to you.'

'You've got a pretty short memory then,' he retaliated. 'Just this morning, on the beach, you said you didn't care what your family thought. You do though, don't you? You care so much that you couldn't bring yourself to admit you were going on holiday with me. The black guy with the embarrassing mother.'

'Don't you start on me!' Anna burst into tears. 'And for God's sake, get rid of that chip on your shoulder! I love you and I want to be with you.'

'But only if you can keep me hidden away so that your family don't find out we're together.' He punched the palm of his hand with his balled-up fist. 'I love you too, Anna – so much. But it can't work if you let other people rule your life.'

'But they don't,' she pleaded. 'Dad told me to go home right now and I told him where to go. I'm staying here with you.'

Felix's face softened slightly. 'You said that? You refused to go?'

Anna nodded, wiping her eyes with her hand.

'And you can hack it? The rows when you do go home, I mean?' Felix asked.

'Of course.'

To her relief, Felix wrapped his arms round her and gave her a hug. 'I'm glad,' he said. 'And I'm sorry if I lost it – it's just that I guess I'm jealous. I want to be the most important person in your life.'

'You know what?' Anna whispered softly. 'You are. You truly are.'

'But darling, you promised to look after your daddy . . . I can rely on you, Anna sweetheart, I know I can . . .'

'I'm just pleased your poor mother isn't around . . .'

'No! Mummy, Dad . . .' Anna shot bolt upright, sweat pouring off her and her heart racing. She stretched out her hand to switch on her bedside light and then remembered. She was on the sofa. She had been tossing and turning for hours and finally gave up any attempt at sleep and had crept downstairs to make a cup of tea. She glanced at the coffee table; the mug of tea was still there, stone cold now of course. She must have dozed off without realising.

The words in her dream were still echoing in her head.

{144}

It had been so real – she had felt as if she could have reached out and touched her mum, her father's rage was as palpable as if he had really been in the room with her.

She flopped back on to the cushions and let the tears flow. Why did it have to be like this? One minute she felt angry with her father for his bigoted, narrow-minded take on life, the next she was wracked with guilt for being the cause of all the trouble he was in. And all the time, her mother's gentle voice was echoing in her head, '*Look after your daddy, look after your daddy.*'

For the first time since her mother's death, a sudden wave of anger swamped her. Her mother had asked too much: looking after Walter wasn't her job. She was seventeen, she had her life ahead of her and her dad would probably be unpredictable till the day he died. Was she supposed to put her life on hold for ever?

She got up from the sofa and opened the kitchen door as quietly as she could. To her horror, the back door was wide open. She froze – and then let out a gasp of relief as she caught sight of Phoebe standing with her back to the house, staring up at the stars.

'Feebs?'

Her friend spun round, and Anna saw at once that she had been crying as well.

'You got the blues, too?' Phoebe came through the door and gave Anna a rueful smile. 'I saw you on the sofa but didn't want to disturb you – not that you looked very peaceful. What's up?'

'You don't want to know,' Anna said and proceeded to tell her the whole story. 'And you?'

'Me and Jamie – it's a total disaster,' Phoebe said. I

should never have come. And tomorrow, I'm going to have to tell him.'

'Tell him what exactly?'

'Look, don't say a word to anyone, right,' Phoebe whispered. 'But I've met someone.'

After ten minutes, during which Phoebe alternately cried, ranted, raved and laughed, Anna discovered that her friend had been to visit her grandmother in Morpeth a few weeks earlier, had travelled back on the train with someone called Cameron, and had fallen passionately in love by the time they'd got as far as York.

'Oh Anna, he's just amazing,' Phoebe said repeatedly. 'He's fit, and witty, and brilliant. We've been out five times since then and —'

'But what about Jamie?' Anna interjected.

'That's the worst part,' Phoebe sighed, her elfin features scrunched up in a frown. 'I had to come on this trip because Zac doesn't know anything about Cameron yet. But being here, when I could be partying with Cameron in London – well, it's just torture.' She closed her eyes. 'Cameron's got his own flat, and a convertible, and he's a member of all these cool clubs that you read about in the style magazines . . .'

'But Jamie adores you and I thought you two were good together,' Anna reasoned.

'I just don't feel anything for him any more,' Phoebe confessed. 'Not now I've seen what it's like to be with a really mature guy.'

Anna laughed in an attempt to lighten the mood. 'I reckon no boy of our age is ever really mature,' she teased. 'That's half the problem.'

'Cameron's thirty.'

For a moment Anna was rendered speechless. 'Thirty? But Phoebe . . .'

'Don't start,' Phoebe snapped. 'He's wonderful, and I love him, and I couldn't give a damn about his age.'

'So what are you going to do about Jamie?' Anna demanded.

'I have to tell him. First thing tomorrow morning. I can't string him along all week and besides, I'm missing Cameron and it's torture not being able to phone him in case Jamie finds out.' She ambled over to the sink. 'Tea?'

Anna nodded.

'But you and Felix, you're OK surely?' Phoebe asked. 'I mean, parents are a pain and all that, but at the end of the day, they can't rule our lives. And you're nearly eighteen – what's your dad on, thinking he can tell you what to do?'

'It's complicated,' Anna replied.

'You mean because of that whole TV business? That's his problem, not yours. Look, my mother will go mental when I tell her about Cameron but tough; it's my life and I'll live it how I want to. And you should do the same.'

She's right, thought Anna, half an hour later as she crept back to bed and tried to go to sleep. *I won't listen to Dad or anyone else. Felix and me, that's all that matters. I'm just going to concentrate on having a good time.*

Which was easier said than done.

On Tuesday, as she was queuing at the ice cream van after an intense game of volleyball on the beach, Anna's mobile beeped. Seeing that it was a voicemail from Marina, and that there had been three missed calls from her that morning, she glanced over her shoulder and, noticing that Felix was busy playing Frisbee with Jamie, she listened to the messages.

'You can ignore my calls all you like but I shan't give up until you speak to me.'

Anna's finger hovered on the *Delete* button.

'I never thought I would say this to you,' her godmother's disembodied voice continued, 'but you are being completely selfish and disloyal to your father – and to your mother's memory.'

Her words felt like a kick in the stomach to Anna whose head was already pounding from the combination of too much Pimm's, a broken night's sleep and an hour of rushing around in the sun.

'Your father wept this morning, Anna – yes, he actually wept. Because of what you've done. I fear for his health; he's been on the edge for weeks, and now this, on top of everything that wretched woman set in motion . . . Words fail me.' They clearly didn't, because she continued without pause. 'Just think, Anna, what your mummy would be saying right now.'

The words were like a knife cutting through Anna's already bruised ego.

'Ring me. Soon. Unless of course you would prefer me to come over there and drag you home and, believe me, I'm tempted!'

Anna snapped the phone shut and shuffled miserably to the head of the queue.

'Six cones with a flake, please,' she muttered, although in truth she doubted she could swallow anything.

She was balancing the cones and edging her way down

the wooden steps back to the beach when her phone beeped again.

'Oh go to . . .!' Why should she spoil the day by phoning Marina? But then, if her dad really was on the edge . . . No, that was just Marina exaggerating. But Marina didn't exaggerate. And her mum had often talked about her father's blustering being a cover for his insecurity.

And what if Marina did turn up at the cottage, which of course, she wouldn't – it was just a threat . . . But what if . . .?

'Anna!' Phoebe grabbed two cones from her hands. 'They're dripping everywhere. And hey, what's up? You look like you've seen a ghost.'

'It's – oh, nothing.'

'Good, because you're going to have to sort Jamie out,' Phoebe muttered. 'I'm about to tell him we're through. And after that I'm catching the five-thirty ferry back. I'm going home.'

For the rest of that day, Anna tried desperately to blot out all thoughts of home. At first it wasn't too hard. Jamie had disappeared soon after Phoebe left and, by ten that evening, he still wasn't back. Felix and Zac had been down to the pub to see if he was drowning his sorrows, but there was no sign of him. He wasn't answering his mobile and his wallet was still on his bed.

Anna, who had left her mobile switched off since Marina's angry phone call, switched it back on and sent a text to Phoebe.

'Just in case he chased after her,' she told the others.

All she got back was an abrupt, *He's big enough to sort*

himself out which she thought was a little harsh under the circumstances.

'He can't do much without any money,' Sula reasoned. 'I guess he just needed some time out. I mean, if Zac did that to me, I'd want to go away, curl up somewhere and just die.'

'But then, I never would,' Zac replied softly, kissing the back of her neck. He turned to Anna. 'You're her friend, has she told you anything? All I got was that she couldn't handle the holiday and she'd explain when I got home.'

'And her timing,' Felix muttered. 'How could she dump him in the middle of a holiday?'

Just then, Anna's phone beeped.

One new message.

'Is it him?' Three voices asked in unison.

It wasn't from Jamie. It was from Mallory.

Dad's in hospital. Please ring. Urgent. M

'Oh my God!' Anna sank into the nearest chair and dialled Mallory's phone.

'What's wrong?' Felix asked.

'It's my dad, he's . . . Mallory? Hi, it's me. What's happened?'

She listened, alarmed and guilty in equal measure, as Mallory told her how, earlier that evening, her father had been ranting about the injustices of his life, and the behaviour of Anna in particular, had stormed out into the garden for a cigar, and been found in a heap in the middle of the lawn.

'They think it's his heart,' Mallory sobbed. 'Gaby's in France and I can't reach her. You have to come home. It's all your fault this has happened.'

{150}

'It's too late to do anything tonight,' Felix said, when Anna had rung off. 'The last ferry will have left ages ago.'

He gave her a hug and Anna rested her head on his chest.

'Mallory thinks it's all my fault,' she sighed.

'Mallory can think what she likes,' Felix replied. 'Whatever is wrong with your dad, it's not down to you. Just get that into your head right now.'

'I'll have to go back,' she ventured. 'First thing in the morning.'

'Of course you do, and I'll take you. This holiday,' he said dryly, 'seems to have been a disaster from the start. Let's hope Zac and Sula manage to come through it unscathed.'

Jamie had returned at midnight, slightly the worse for drink and acting in a way that convinced all of them, if they had needed any convincing, that drama was definitely the most appropriate career for him. The following morning Anna, Felix and Jamie – who was hell bent on chasing after Phoebe who he said was 'a flower in a field of weeds' – left for Fleckford.

The closer they got to home, the more anxious Anna became. Felix had been great, sorting out the ferry, doing all the driving and insisting on stopping for lunch because he said hospital visiting couldn't be done on an empty stomach. Jamie had insisted on getting the fast train direct to London despite not having a clue where Phoebe would be hanging out, and after trying to dissuade him Felix had given in and dropped him off at Southampton station. For the remainder of the journey he had kept up a stream of chat.

'I know it's a lot to ask,' Anna ventured, as Felix pulled up in the hospital car park, switched off the ignition and opened the car door, 'but will you come in with me? I'm not very good in hospitals and . . .'

'Of course I'll come,' he replied, squeezing her hand.

Walter was in a side room and Anna could hear his voice from way down the corridor.

'Good sign,' Felix teased. 'He hasn't lost the power of speech.'

Gingerly, she pushed open the door. A tall, grey-haired man in a dark suit, whom she assumed was the consultant, was standing at the foot of the bed. Walter, looking strangely vulnerable in a hospital gown, was propped up on pillows.

'. . . not a heart attack at all,' the consultant was saying. 'You'd clearly been hitting the bottle rather too much . . .'

'Are you suggesting . . .?'

'. . . and that,' the consultant continued calmly, 'plus what was undoubtedly an angina attack caused you to pass out. And you also have very high blood pressure which . . .'

At that moment, Walter turned and caught sight of Anna and Felix, who were hovering in the doorway.

'High blood pressure, you say? Well, it'll be a damn sight higher if you don't get that boy out of my room right now!'

'Dad, that's not fair – if it wasn't for Felix, I wouldn't have got here half as quickly . . .'

'If it wasn't for your sordid little romance with Felix, I wouldn't have encountered that woman and I wouldn't be in here,' her father stormed. He turned to the doctor. 'Stress, you said – that's what I'm suffering from?'

'It could certainly be a contributing factor, but the alcohol, your smoking . . .'

'Satisfied?' He glared at Anna.

'I'll leave you to your visitors,' the doctor said. 'And I'll sign your release papers. But you need to see your GP and get this angina sorted and make some fairly major lifestyle changes.'

'You heard what the doctor said? Major lifestyle changes, or my health will go downhill.'

Three hours later, Walter was home, holding court while Araminta, who had sped up the motorway the moment she heard the news, sat on the arm of the sofa, stroking his balding head as if he were a child of two.

'You must drink less,' Marina said sternly. 'Party less and accept that you're not getting any younger.'

'Well, if my own daughter wasn't driving me to drink, it might be easier,' he sighed, slipping into the role of the much misjudged, ill-treated parent. 'I want you to keep away from that boy, Anna – at least till all this business with his mother is sorted. The lawyers are meeting next month and I can't afford to . . .'

His voice faltered and his eyes filled with tears.

'If it all goes horribly wrong, I'll have let your mum down and I can't bear that.'

That was what did it. In that moment, Anna knew she had to help her father through this, whatever it took. And he did say 'till this business is sorted'.

She knew what she had to do. And how she could, despite everything, make it bearable.

'How's he doing?'

Felix had driven to their place in the woods as soon as

Anna, confident that her father's trip with Marina to the GP would take at least an hour, phoned him the following morning. He had picked her up, whirled her round and round and kissed her full on the lips.

'Now your Dad's home, how about we try to redeem our week? I don't mean go back to the cottage, but I thought we could . . .'

'We can't do anything,' Anna said, her voice shaking slightly. 'For the time being, we've got to see less of each other.'

For a moment, the only sound was the chirping of the birds and the rustling of leaves in the beech trees.

'Say that again.' Felix's voice was tight with emotion.

'Oh, I'm not dumping you,' Anna assured him hastily, taking his hand. 'Just saying that when we meet, we've got to do it in secret. I'll tell my dad that I am doing things his way – not seeing you till all this mess with your mum is sorted – and then we'll arrange how we can get together when he's out of the way . . .'

'So hang on, let me get this straight.' Felix snatched his hand away. 'You want us to have a secret relationship? Behind closed doors?'

'Well, yes – I mean I can say I've got band rehearsals and parties with friends and . . .'

'Anna, Anna.' Felix cupped her face in his hands. 'You just don't get it, do you?'

'What do you mean?'

'I love you – and I want the whole world to know just how much you mean to me. This idea of hiding away – it's like we're ashamed of what we feel for one another. No way am I going to hide in a corner.'

'But if we just keep Dad calm —'

'It's not up to you to keep him calm, Anna. If you do this, what will happen next? Two years down the line, you'll make another decision he doesn't like and then what?'

Anna took his hand. 'I promise, it's just for a few weeks. Then when this court case business is all sorted . . .'

'And what if the case goes against him? What then?'

For a moment Anna was lost for words.

'I love you. You know that. But I can't and won't lie – I can't be two-faced. And I won't dance to someone else's tune.' He touched her cheek. 'You told me that I was the most important person in your life.'

'You are, but . . .'

'It doesn't look that way to me. I can't do this, Anna. It's best if we face facts. It's over between us.'

And with that he turned and strode up the path. She ran after him, pleading, crying, telling him he'd got it all wrong, believing that any minute, he would turn back, take her in his arms and tell her that, if keeping things quiet for a bit would make her happy, then he'd do it.

But that didn't happen.

As he reached his car, she grabbed his arm. He paused, and turned to face her, and she saw that his eyes were glistening with unshed tears. 'I loved you so much, Anna,' he whispered. 'And I thought you felt the same.'

Choking back the tears, she tried to reply but before she could utter a word he had got into his car and driven away.

❧ CHAPTER 12 ❧

*'It is a sort of pain, too, which is new to me. I have been
used to the gratification of believing myself to earn
every blessing that I enjoyed.'*
(Jane Austen, *Persuasion*)

SHE HAD SENT EMAILS. SHE HAD BOMBARDED HIM WITH text messages. She had even written long letters. She had prayed harder than she had ever prayed in her life.

And she heard nothing from him.

The only news she got came via Phoebe.

'Zac says the best thing you can do is butt out for now,' she told Anna. 'Apparently, when he quizzed Felix about what happened between you two, he just said that no way was he going to let you stab him through the heart again. That's really poetic, isn't it? For a boy, I mean?'

Anna had no option but to pin all her hopes on Christmas. Phoebe had told her that Zac and Felix would be home on Christmas Eve for ten days. On Shannon's advice, she tried to change everything about her old self: she had her hair cut into a feathery bob, let it return to its natural colour, got herself a French manicure, and blew more cash than she should have on clothes.

'See, the important thing,' Shannon, who was very into psychology at the time, explained, 'is to surprise him with the new look which tells his subconscious mind that you are now different in outlook as well as in the way you look. Clever, eh? I read it in *Psychologies* magazine.'

Anna began to have high hopes, but on Christmas Eve, she went down with flu. On Boxing Day, Phoebe sent her a text.

Zac and Felix going skiing 2moro. F spending 2nite at our place. Over 2 u!

'What are you doing?' Mallory demanded a couple of hours later as Anna, white as a sheet, staggered downstairs, wearing her coat, scarf and gloves and clutching a gift-wrapped package. 'You're ill. And don't come near me – I don't want your germs.'

'I'm going out for a breath of fresh air,' Anna replied. 'It'll make me feel . . .'

What it was going to make her feel, Mallory was never to find out. Anna had fainted on the hall floor.

'You wouldn't have wanted him to see you looking like road kill,' Shannon remarked the following day, when Anna sobbed out the story on the phone.

'Tell you what – you said he'd be qualifying or passing out or whatever they call it next month, right? Get the Harvilles to take you along to the ceremony.'

'I suppose.'

'And when you're there, you tell him that from now on you won't let your father rule your life,' her friend concluded.

'I wish it were that simple,' Anna sighed.

'Anna Eliot, life is as simple or as difficult as you choose to make it,' Shannon declared. 'Just do it!

To: feebsharville@btinternet.com
From: saxygirl@tiscali.net
*Hi Feebs! Is Felix's passing out ceremony open to anyone?
Do you think it would be all right if I tagged along? I'd really
like to see him . . .*

For two days she didn't get a reply. When she did, she
wished she hadn't.

To: saxygirl@tiscali.net
From: feebsharville@btinternet.com
*Hi! Thanks for the email. We checked with Zac about
arrangements. He said it would be best to leave it. Sorry, babe.
But I'll put in a good word for you with Felix, OK? Must dash
– Cameron's taking me to RockFest at the Bowl.*

The mention of a rock concert reminded Anna about
the tickets she had given to Felix for *Sugar Lumps* at O_2.
Who, she wondered miserably, would he go with now? She
didn't have to wait long for an answer. The next day, she
found an envelope on the doormat addressed to her in
Felix's looping scrawl.

For a moment, she dared to hope.

She ripped open the letter. The two tickets to the
concert fell out at her feet.

*This would have been fun. Guess you can find someone
more suitable to go along with. F*

That was when she fully realised the extent to which
she had hurt him. And resigned herself to never getting
him back.

Ironically, just a few weeks later, Anna's father was persuaded by his lawyer that continuing to hold out and make a scene was not wise. He made a substantial donation to the Alzheimer's charity (the world didn't have to know that it was Marina's money, since his own finances were frozen until his creditors had been satisfied) and Cassandra, following a muted apology in the press, accepted that this matter was closed.

None of which made Anna feel in the slightest bit better.

PART TWO

❧ CHAPTER 13 ❧

'How much handsomer, how infinitely more agreeable
they thought him than any individual among
their male acquaintance!'
(Jane Austen, *Persuasion*)

'COME ON, COME ON, GET A MOVE ON!'

Anna tapped the steering wheel in irritation as she was forced to crawl along the road into Kellynch village behind a grindingly slow tractor and trailer. It was only a few days until the Fleckford Music Festival, and she had a thousand things to do. The band wasn't up to scratch with their pieces, she still hadn't finished preparing for her first session with the summer school kids at the theatre the following day, and to cap it all, Marina, who was about to leave for her ten-day trip to Madeira, had given her a huge box of tombola prizes to drop off at Uppercross Farm on her way to rehearse at Mia's place.

'For pity's sake, pull over!' Anna shouted, her hands gripping the steering wheel. Her stomach was turning over and over, her chest was tight, and she had to fight the urge to burst into tears.

And she knew deep down that none of it had anything

to do with the crawling tractor ahead of her.

Felix was home. He and Zac had been back in England for ten whole days. They'd both been checked over and discharged from Selly Oak Hospital; Zac was back with his mum and Phoebe, and Felix had been staying with Cassandra in her new flat in Bythorn, but today he would be arriving at Hampton House. What's more, he would be staying with Ruth for at least a month while he had physio three times a week at Stoke Mandeville hospital.

She knew all this from Phoebe, who had been nagging her for days to get her act together.

'You're nuts,' she had said a few days earlier. 'Zac's been to see him three times – even I went yesterday. And what do you do? Nothing.'

'You don't understand,' Anna had sighed.

'Too right I don't,' her friend agreed. 'I mean, if it was Cameron, I'd do anything to get to him.'

'Yes, but you two are still together,' Anna pointed out.

'Despite my mother's best efforts, yes we are,' laughed Phoebe. 'Honestly, Anna, he's so gorgeous and do you know what he did last week? He bought me . . .'

Anna was so used to hearing Phoebe eulogising about Cameron that she switched off mentally and let her carry on. When she finally paused for breath, Anna voiced the question that had been plaguing her ever since he got home.

'Did – did Felix mention me at all when you were there?'

There was only a slight pause but it was long enough to tell Anna what she needed to know.

'He didn't, right?' she asked.

'Well, no, but then boys don't talk about the things that

really matter do they? Just go and see him, OK?'

But Anna hadn't gone. And she knew why – because if she went to see Felix and he didn't want to know, all her hopes would be dashed. Better to wait and pray that, when he saw her around the village or playing at the Festival, all the old feelings would come to the surface and he'd realise that he needed to be with her.

Like that was really going to happen.

The tractor finally turned into a farm track, and Anna pressed down on the accelerator and roared the last half mile down to Uppercross Farm, startling chickens and the farm cat as she turned into the yard and squealed to a halt outside the back door. Bunting was stretched across the farmyard, and a huge poster advertising pony rides and trailer tours had been stuck into the lawn by the tearoom in readiness for the Festival.

Staggering under the weight of the box of tombola prizes, hardly able to see where she was going, Anna kicked open the permanently unlocked back door. Her foot hit something soft, something that yelped loudly – and she felt herself stumble. The box flew out of her hands and she landed heavily on the quarry-tiled floor.

'Anna!'

She looked up. It was as though for an instant the entire room was in freeze-frame. Bea, with her hands clasped to her mouth in horror; Ruth Croft, hand outstretched to take a slice of shortbread; Charlie, Mallory and Louisa stifling laughter, Henrietta, can of cola halfway to her lips, plus a slightly disgruntled dog that had now retreated to a safe distance.

And Felix. Felix, his right cheek partially covered in

gauze, his left hand strapped in bandages and two fingers in plaster, was sitting somewhat awkwardly in the pine chair on the far side of the huge kitchen table staring straight into her eyes.

This wasn't how it was meant to be. She'd planned everything so carefully – what she would be wearing, how she would behave, even the words she would say to Felix. Anna got up very slowly.

'Lulu, get the arnica,' Bea ordered Louisa. 'She's got a nasty bruise coming up already. And Henrietta, don't just stand there – pick up those things.'

She patted Anna's hand.

'You look exhausted, darling,' she fussed. 'Mind you, with all that's been going on these last few weeks I'm hardly surprised, losing your home and . . .'

She stopped short, glancing with embarrassment in Ruth's direction.

'Oh, and of course you know Felix,' Bea gabbled.

'Hi,' Anna murmured, conscious that Felix was now averting his gaze.

'You two know each other?' Ruth asked Anna. 'Well why didn't you say so before?'

'Maybe she didn't think it was important.' The tone of Felix's voice was like a knife plunged straight into Anna's guts.

'They say Felix might get a medal for bravery,' Bea rattled on, taking the tube of arnica cream from Louisa and patting some on Anna's cheekbone. 'Isn't that wonderful?'

'That's a long way off,' Felix said hastily. 'If it happens at all.'

'You said you had to go back to Plymouth in a bit for a

{166}

parade and medals,' Ruth pointed out.

'Those are campaign medals,' Felix explained. 'Zac'll get one – all of them will. Anything else comes later.'

'You were so amazing,' Louisa enthused. 'I've been watching all the news reports.'

'And I cut out all the bits in the newspapers about you,' Henrietta cut in. 'I've never met a real hero before.'

'Charlie's my hero, aren't you?' Mallory chipped in, clearly anxious not to be left out. She slipped her hand through his arm and pouted in the way that always gave Anna the urge to throw up on the spot.

'Talking of Zac, how is he?' Anna asked, hoping to engage Felix in some sort of conversation.

'He's gone down to Dorset – Sula's family have a house at Lyme Regis,' he said, still talking to the room at large rather than look at Anna. 'It'll do him good – he's been really low lately.'

'Not surprising after what you've all been through,' Ruth commented. 'Could it be PTSD?'

'Hopefully not,' Felix replied quietly.

'What's that?' Henrietta asked anxiously. 'Is it like MRSA?'

'Don't be stupid,' Louisa retorted. 'It's post-traumatic stress disorder. That's right, isn't it, Felix?'

She sidled closer to him and he nodded, fiddling with the spoon in his coffee mug.

'A few days unwinding with Sula and he'll be fine,' Bea said cheerfully. 'So all's well that end's well.'

'Tell that to the poor sods still stuck out there,' Felix muttered under his breath. For an instant he caught Anna's eye and, just as quickly, averted his gaze and got to his feet, wincing slightly as he eased his hand into a more comfortable position.

'Roo, we should get going,' he said.

'Coming, sir!' Ruth gave him a mock salute, kissed Bea and followed him to the door, pausing to glance at Anna.

For a moment Felix's eyes met Anna's and then just as quickly he looked away and strode across the yard.

'Oh my God, he is so hot!' Louisa exclaimed.

'And available,' Henrietta added.

'You've got Leo,' her sister snapped back.

'If you don't mind, I must get going,' Anna murmured. 'Workshop at the theatre.'

So that's it, she thought. *We've met and he obviously hasn't forgiven me. Whatever Louisa does or doesn't do, Felix and I are over. He can't stand to be in the same room as me. I'm still hung up on him after all this time – I should have got over him by now. What kind of idiot was I to ever think I was in with a chance?*

'I am so annoyed!' Mallory had appeared on the doorstep of Magpie Cottage within minutes of Anna arriving home after her workshop session at the theatre the following day. She was starving hungry and yearning to sink into a hot bath. The last thing she needed was for her sister to off-load her troubles.

'Why?' she asked wearily because she knew it was expected of her.

'It's Charlie and this stupid chariot race for the Festival,' Mallory said. 'We were supposed to be going to the cinema this evening, but oh no! You know why?'

'Since I'm not psychic, no I don't,' Anna snapped. 'And

shouldn't you be at the tearoom? I thought they stayed open till six.'

'They do, but honestly, they treat me like a slave,' Mallory moaned. 'You know what – they expect me to clean tables and wash the floor at the end of the day, and sterilise all the stuff and . . .'

'That's what a job is, Mallory,' Anna retorted. 'The grot as well as the good bits.'

'Yeah, yeah,' Mallory said dismissively. 'Anyway, about Charlie – he's got it into his head that he's going to tart up that old go-kart in the barn and enter the race. He's got Felix roped in and . . .'

To Anna's irritation her undisciplined heart still lurched at the sound of that name.

'Felix?' she asked as nonchalantly as she could.

'Yeah, Charlie mentioned it yesterday, before you turned up, and asked for help. Then Felix rang and said he was up for it. So now the two of them are holed up in the barn behaving like ten-year-olds.'

'But his hand . . .'

'Doesn't appear to stop him giving instructions on aerodynamics, or whatever you call it,' Mallory said. 'And hey, do you know what he said about you? He said you looked so different that, if he'd passed you in the street, he wouldn't have recognised you.'

And I would know him among a thousand guys even if I hadn't seen him for twenty years, Anna thought sadly.

'It's the hair, I guess,' she commented hurriedly.

'And the fact that you've lost weight,' Mallory said. 'Your face has gone all gaunt and bony.'

'Oh thanks,' Anna said.

'Anyway, none of that is why I came,' Mallory went on. 'Dad called.'

'And?'

'He's having a housewarming party in a couple of weeks and we've all got to be there or else,' she said. 'Drinks in the apartment and then food at the Yacht Club. Araminta's organising it.'

'Why,' Anna sighed, 'doesn't that surprise me?'

'Do you think,' Mallory ventured, 'that her and dad will – well, you know?'

'I think they probably "you know" already,' Anna muttered.

'No, I mean get married,' Mallory replied. 'I reckon they'll announce it at this party.'

'No way!' Anna cried. 'I mean, getting together is one thing but getting married? He'd never do that – I mean, Mum was everything to him and . . .'

'Mum's not here,' Mallory reminded her. 'And Araminta is.'

❧ CHAPTER 14 ❧

'Her imagination and her heart were bewitched.'
(Jane Austen, *Persuasion*)

'THIS VOLUNTEERING IS PRETTY EXHAUSTING, ISN'T IT?'

Shannon wheeled her chair over to the table where Anna was packing up percussion instruments at the end of the Friday afternoon workshop session. 'Fun, though,' she added, as parents drifted in to pick up their children. 'One of the kids in my group is really talented and . . . Anna, are you listening?'

'What? Oh sorry. I was just thinking.'

'Worrying more like, judging by the expression on your face,' Shannon remarked. 'Go on, have one of these and spill the beans.'

She shoved a packet of chocolate biscuits in Anna's face.

'The Musgroves are having a barbecue tonight,' Anna said. 'They do it every year before the Festival – a kind of buttering up for the people in the village who might be put out by the noise and stuff. And they want me to be there.'

'This does not seem to be a cause for calling an emergency summit,' Shannon teased.

'Felix might be there. He and Charlie seem to be getting pretty friendly.'

'Great!' Shannon cried. 'So what's your plan?'

'Shannon, for goodness' sake, can't you get it into your head that it's going nowhere? He's seen me three times – once at the Musgroves and twice round the village now and if he'd wanted to talk he would have done.'

'Guys operate differently from us,' Shannon said calmly, totally ignoring her friend's outburst. 'You have to drip-feed them – if he keeps seeing you, all the old memories and love and lust will resurface. Trust me. I know.'

'You do?'

'There's this guy I know – he lives near my gran and . . .'

'You kept that pretty quiet!'

'Yes, well – that's because he asked me out last year and I said no. He took offence and now I really want him to ask again and he hasn't. It'll be the same with Felix – but you have to keep at it.'

Anna laughed. 'OK, OK, point taken,' she said. 'Thing is, even if I do go . . . oh my God!'

She turned as a blood-curdling scream emanated from the far corner of the room. Alfie Green, one of her favourite children in the group, was sobbing in terror as blood streamed from his nose. Amanda, the thirty-something group leader, was standing beside him as white as a sheet dabbing ineffectually with a paper tissue.

Within seconds Shannon and Anna were at his side, just as Amanda announced she was going to faint and promptly did so. For a while chaos reigned; parents ushered their children away, the other leader, Anthony, went in search of ice, Anna held the boy's hand and tried to calm him while Shannon, who had a first-aid qualification, told him what to do. Amanda came round, took one look at Alfie and fled the room, stating she was about to throw up.

Fifteen minutes later, the blood was still pumping. And Alfie's mum was nowhere to be seen.

'Ambulance,' decided Anthony, a remark that caused little Alfie to screech even louder. 'And phone his mum again. Where the hell is she? Pick-up time was ages ago.'

Half an hour later, Anna found herself sitting in the ambulance with Alfie and Anthony heading for Fleckford Hospital A&E.

'She can't go,' Shannon had said when Anthony pointed out that Child Protection demanded two people be with Alfie. 'She's got a date. I'll go.'

'Sorry, love,' said the paramedic, gesturing to her chair. 'But we can't . . .'

'It's OK,' Anna said. 'It'll be fine. I'll have plenty of time to get back here on the bus, pick up my car and get home to change. And if I don't, it's no big deal.'

Only as the minutes ticked by, the more of a big deal it felt. Anthony had left countless messages on Alfie's mother's phone but she still hadn't turned up. Alfie had been seen by a doctor who declared that, unless the bleeding stopped within another half-hour, he would have to pack his nose with gauze.

'You go,' Anthony said to Anna. 'I'll stay with Alfie.'

But every time Anna made to leave, Alfie burst into more sobs. Anna stayed; she stayed while his nose was packed with gauze, she stayed and told him stories until he fell into a restless fitful sleep.

At eight o'clock, Alfie's mother finally appeared, dishevelled and flushed, her cheeks smudged with mascara and her eyes red. 'So so sorry, my car broke down on this side road miles from anywhere, and I had no credit on the phone and by the time I'd walked to the nearest village . . .'

Anna fled, glancing at her watch and deciding to grab a cab whatever the expense. The taxi rank was empty. When she did flag down a passing cab, it seemed that every set of traffic lights were against them, and every slow-moving vehicle had decided to take the same route.

R u there yet? Shannon texted as the cab crawled along behind a muck spreader.

No – 2 l8. No time 2 change. Not going, she texted back.

Don't u dare – such a cop out! Go as u r. Or u will have me 2 answer 2.

Anna glanced down at her less than spotless white jeans and totally unflattering trainers, neither of which would have been her first choice of what to wear. But, she reminded herself sternly, since any chance of getting back with Felix was out of the question, it didn't really matter. No one would notice or care anyway.

He wasn't there.

Anna stood by the wrought-iron gate that led to the Musgroves' garden and scanned the scene. Groups of people from the village, all of whom Anna recognised, were chatting in huddles under the umbrellas and gazebos that dotted the lawn. Charlie and Zac were sprawled on the grass, drinking from cans of beer, Henrietta and Leo were popping bits of sausage into one another's mouths, and Louisa was sitting on the swinging hammock seat talking in an animated fashion to Phoebe.

'You came, then?'

She wheeled round and there he was, standing behind her, holding a frisbee in his good hand.

'Louisa reckoned you wouldn't come,' he said, frowning slightly. 'What on earth happened to you?'

'I – er – I got held up,' she stammered.

'Doing what?'

'I help out at a music workshop,' she said. 'And this kid . . .'

'Over here, Felix!' Louisa jumped up and beckoned enthusiastically.

'Coming!' he called back and then turned to face Anna.

'It must be a pretty dangerous workshop,' he said, just the merest trace of a smile twitching at the corners of his mouth. 'You do know you've got blood all down the back of your T-shirt?' He paused. 'Seriously, you're not hurt are you?'

At least he spoke to me, Anna thought as she raided Mallory's wardrobe for a clean top. *He could have just walked past. Was he being polite, pointing out the blood to stop me from being embarrassed? That shows he must care. Doesn't it? Please God, let him want me back again.*

'Anna, I've got something so amazing to tell you!' Phoebe burst into the room, glancing briefly over her shoulder. 'Look!'

She plunged her hand down her shirt and pulled out a ring on a chain.

'Cameron and me – we're engaged!'

'You're what?' Anna's mouth dropped open and she stared at Phoebe in disbelief.

'You mustn't breathe a word to a soul,' Phoebe ordered her. 'I mean, Louisa and Hen know but —'

'Which means that by tomorrow the whole of Facebook and half of Twitter will be on the case,' Anna interrupted. 'But Phoebe – what does your mum say?'

'I haven't told her yet,' Phoebe said. 'That's why I can't wear the ring. It's kind of tricky. She doesn't approve of Cameron. Neither does Zac. But that's just because they are so prejudiced.'

'About what?'

'His age, his lifestyle, the fact that he's been married before . . . Well, still is, kind of, but . . .'

'Married?' Anna gasped. 'But . . .'

'It happens,' Phoebe butted in defensively. 'It wasn't his fault. And the divorce will be through soon. Poor guy, he says that Alison was so controlling . . .'

'Phoebe, you're crazy – I mean, what about uni?'

Phoebe looked sheepish.

'Don't tell me . . . Oh come on, you are still going?'

'Cameron says there's no point,' Phoebe said. 'Like, he's got so many contacts and he can get me a job at the drop of a hat. Not that I'll need to work.'

Anna stood there, open-mouthed, shaking her head.

'Well, aren't you going to congratulate me?' Phoebe asked. 'Or is it that you're jealous?'

'Of course it's not. I think you're mad but I guess if it's what you really want, then good luck – and congratulations! Does Jamie know?'

Phoebe looked at her and frowned. 'No – why would he?'

'You'll have to tell him before he hears it from the twins. You owe him that at least.'

'Why? He's nothing to me any more.'

'No, but you're a hell of a lot to him. He'll be home in a couple of days . . . I met his mum in town and she told me. He's been doing loads of auditions and he's landed a part in *The Bill*. He's coming back for a break before filming starts.'

'Let's hope that gets him off my back then,' Phoebe retorted. 'He's still sending emails and cards and soppy poems. Sad or what?'

'That's what people do when they really care,' Anna sighed. She turned to leave and then paused. 'And you will tell your mum? And Zac?' At least, she thought, they might be able to make her see sense.

'Soon,' Phoebe said. 'When Cameron can come up and hold my hand. Not that it will make any difference. I'm not like you; I know what I want and no way am I changing my mind because of something my mother says.' She flicked her hair over her shoulders and looked at Anna. 'I would have thought you would understand that more than anyone.'

Following her down into the garden, Anna had to acknowledge that she had a point.

❧ CHAPTER 15 ❧

'If I was wrong in yielding to persuasion once,
remember that it was to persuasion exerted
on the side of safety, not of risk. When I yielded,
I thought it was to duty . . .'
(Jane Austen, *Persuasion*)

THE FESTIVAL WAS IN FULL SWING. THE CHARIOT RACE had
been a great success, although Charlie's kart lost a wheel on
Stocks Hill, and he and Felix ended up pushing it to the
finishing post, Felix using only his good hand and some very
colourful language. The carnival procession had wound its
way through the villages of Kellynch and Drayton Magna,
the fancy-dress competition was underway in the Memorial
Gardens and, at Hampton House, Wild Chicks were
nearing the end of their one-hour slot.

For Anna, it was a surreal experience; the band was
playing on the verandah that had, until so recently, been
as familiar to her as the rest of her home, but was now
bedecked, not with urns full of the trailing fuchsias her
mother had loved so much, but with Japanese Cheya
lanterns, a couple of sculpted heads in marble and a
tinkling water feature of the variety that her father

would be sure to call naff.

The lawn, which had once been mown to bowling-green precision, was sprouting daisies and dandelions and several oriental wind chimes had been hung from the trees by the shepherd's hut. The whole place was swarming with people, eating cream teas, admiring the garden or simply lounging around listening to the music and enjoying the continuing heat wave.

Twice she had played a wrong note because she had allowed her eyes to scan the garden in the hope of catching sight of Felix, although why she was putting herself through the agony, she couldn't work out.

It was halfway through 'Hang On To My Heart' that she looked up briefly and there he was, leaning against an apple tree and staring straight at her. Their eyes met and he didn't look away. A breeze caught the corner of her sheet music and she reached out to secure it. When she looked up, he had turned away, and was laughing out loud, that deep, throaty laugh she remembered so well.

And the girl whose hand he was taking and who was gazing up at him with wide-eyed adoration, was Louisa Musgrove.

'Anna?'

The band had ended its session and Anna was about to follow the others in search of cold drinks, when Ruth touched her on the shoulder.

'Look,' Ruth began before Anna had the chance to open her mouth. 'I don't have a clue about the ins and outs of what went on between you and Felix, but I do know this.'

Anna waited for the verbal onslaught that she felt sure was coming.

'You're clearly much loved round here – and when us old fogies interfere in the lives of you young people, it very often ends in tears,' she declared. 'I can only guess at what went on between you and Felix – he won't talk about it.'

She shielded her eyes from the sun with her hand and glanced down the garden. 'Interestingly though, when I suggested that he might like Joseph and me to take him away somewhere for a bit, he was very quick to say he wanted to hang around here.'

She nodded in the direction of where Louisa and Felix were still laughing and joking together. 'He seems to be making friends,' she commented. 'Mind you, he won't find it easy.'

'Sorry – what do you mean?'

Ruth smiled. 'I've spent all my married life travelling the world with Joseph,' she explained. 'And you know what? I think that back home, I probably have two friends. Lots of acquaintances, of course, but just two friends.' She looked at Anna, her smile fading. 'It takes a very special kind of person to sustain a friendship across long distances,' she said. 'They say life is always easier for the person going away than for the one left behind.' She looked again at Felix. 'But you know, I've never been sure that is true at all. Sometimes you come home with such expectations, such hopes . . . Oh there you are, Joseph darling! Did you get the ice cubes?'

The moment was broken and Anna was left to reflect on what Ruth had actually been trying to say.

* * *

'Anna? Hi, how are you doing?'

Anna was about to get into her car to drive back to Magpie Cottage and change for the ceilidh when she heard the familiar voice.

'Jamie! You're back – great to see you. Congratulations, by the way – you must be over the moon.'

'About what?'

'The TV part,' Anna replied.

'Oh. Yes. Thanks. Have you heard that Phoebe's got . . .' His voice faltered.

'Engaged?' Anna asked gently. 'She told you then?'

'No, I overheard Henrietta and Leo talking, and I caught the words "Phoebe" and "engagement" – so I got Leo to tell me. I just can't bear it.'

His jaw was grinding and he looked as if he was about to burst into tears.

'I know it must be hard, but you've not been together for some time now and . . .'

'Anna, when you love like I love, you don't get over it,' Jamie said dramatically. 'I'll never find another girl like Phoebe, never.'

'Of course you will, and one who will treat you better,' Anna replied resolutely. 'The theatrical world must be full of great girls.'

'None as great as Feebs.'

Time, Anna thought, *for a change of conversation.*

'Are you coming to the ceilidh tonight?'

'I don't know that I can bear it – not if Phoebe's going to be there.'

'She's not, she's gone back to London.'

'To be with him, I suppose,' Jamie sighed.

'Come,' Anna said firmly. 'And that's an order, OK? I'm relying on you.'

Normally, Anna loved to dance but she simply couldn't get in the mood. Jamie had turned up and then sat, morose and silent, by the bar staring into space, Louisa monopolised Felix, and Henrietta was all over Leo. She had hoped Shannon and the others would stay for the evening, but they had other plans.

Anna was in the loo, which was really a Portakabin outside the parish hall, when she heard familiar voices through the open skylight window.

'If Mallory moans one more time about nobody eating her flaming flapjacks this afternoon, I'll scream.'

That was Louisa.

'Honestly, how Charlie puts up with her, I'll never know,' she went on. 'She's so stuck up, just like Gaby. Anna's OK – although she's a bit of a pushover. But then, from what I hear, you know all about that.'

Anna held her breath. Louisa must be talking to Felix.

'I'll tell you what, though,' she said. 'No one on earth would make me do something I didn't want to do. Mum tries from time to time but she usually gives up with me. Hen is far more obedient!'

She laughed and Anna could just imagine the effect that those immaculately even white teeth, and that flawless skin and her piercingly blue eyes would have on Felix.

'But talking about Anna, you know what my mum says? She thinks . . .'

What her mother thought, Anna was never to discover because Louisa's words were drowned out by someone banging on the loo door and demanding to know whether Anna had died in there. She stood at the washbasin, letting water trickle over her hands and gazing in the mirror in a trance. A pushover? Was that how people saw her? It wasn't true – and how could Louisa say such a thing to Felix of all people?

As she wandered disconsolately back into the hall, Henrietta came bounding up to her, closely followed by Leo, balancing two over-full glasses of wine.

'Anna, wait! Isn't it amazing? I can't wait, can you?' She grabbed Anna by the arm. 'At first Mum wasn't going to let me and Lou go, but . . .'

'Hen, I don't have the remotest idea what you are on about,' Anna sighed, not really in the mood to play along.

'Didn't Zac call you?' Henrietta frowned. 'He and Sula are having this kind of house party next weekend. It's so cool.'

Anna was about to reply when, out of the corner of her eye, she spotted Louisa and Felix coming back into the hall, hand in hand.

'It's going to be great,' Henrietta babbled on. 'He said he'd invite Leo and me, of course, Charlie and Mallory, Louisa and Felix . . .'

So their names are coupled together already, Anna thought, feeling sick and tearful at the same time.

'He probably won't invite me,' Anna said quickly, playing for time.

'Don't be silly, of course he will,' Henrietta said. 'Zac likes you a lot.' She paused, glancing over to the bar where Jamie was still sitting, slumped over a lager. 'And Jamie, of course,' she said, 'so it won't all be couples.'

'Are you going to Zac's?' Felix asked Anna a few moments later while the others were dancing.

'I'm not sure.' She wanted to add 'Do you want me to?' but didn't dare.

'So what's the problem?' Felix asked. 'Do you have to ask your father's permission to attend a party where I'm going to be a guest?'

'No,' Anna said wearily. 'And you know what? Your snide remarks are getting very boring. I kind of think *you're* the one who needs to grow up.'

With that, she turned and walked out of the hall. She couldn't believe she'd said that, but she realised that she meant it. As she reached her car, her hands were shaking so much that she could hardly get the key into the lock. As she fumbled she heard footsteps behind her. Turning, she came face to face with Felix.

'I'm sorry,' he said and then he grinned. 'But I'm glad I made that stupid remark.'

'Really? I can't think why.'

'Because,' he said, '*I saw a glimpse of my feisty Anna.* Anyway, gotta go – promised to walk the twins home.'

She sat in the car for several minutes before switching on the ignition. And all the way back to Magpie Cottage, one phrase kept reverberating round and round in her head.

'My *feisty* Anna. My *feisty* Anna.'

My Anna.

It was probably just a slip of the tongue, she thought. *But I was once his. And what he doesn't realise is that I still am. And somehow, it feels like I always will be.*

❧ CHAPTER 16 ❧

'What is to be done next?
What, in heaven's name, is to be done next?'
(Jane Austen, *Persuasion*)

'COOL PLACE THIS, ISN'T IT?'

It was late on Friday afternoon, and all of them, along with a handful of Sula's mates, were hanging out in the garden at Wings, Sula's house, overlooking the harbour at Lyme Regis. They were drinking Pimm's and making plans when a tall, fair-haired guy with an almost too perfect suntan came and flopped down on the grass beside Anna.

'Hi there!' he said. 'I'm Hugo – Hugo Fanshawe.'

'Anna Eliot,' Anna smiled. 'So – are you a friend of Sula?'

'We were at school together – Eastbourne College,' he replied. 'Then she went to uni in Newcastle, I went to Brighton and we haven't seen one another for months. I see she's got a new boyfriend.'

He nodded in their direction; Zac was standing, arm draped round Sula's shoulder, talking to Jamie and Felix.

'You live in Eastbourne?' Anna queried. 'My dad's just moved there – to Sovereign Harbour.'

'Hey, small world!' Hugo said. 'My parents live at Alfriston – we've got a boat at Sovereign Harbour. We must get together and I'll take you sailing!'

His confidence both irritated and fascinated Anna. And he was extremely good-looking.

'So do you know the Hendersons? And the Dalrymples? They're friends of my dad's.'

'Come sailing with me, and I'll introduce you to the right crowd,' Hugo replied. 'Proper sailors, none of this messing about on Sundays as long as the wind isn't more than force three!'

Despite his sarcastic tone, she couldn't help smiling. Her father had often said the same thing about weekend sailors, saying that the only thing worse was weekend drivers towing caravans.

'By the way, are you here with someone?' Hugo asked.

'Yes, I came with the Musgroves – that's Charlie over there, and . . .'

'I meant, are you *with* someone,' he emphasised. 'A boyfriend.'

Anna paused, watching out of the corner of her eye as Louisa, glass in hand, perched herself on Felix's knee. 'No,' she said quietly. 'No, I'm not.'

'This weekend,' Hugo said, 'is looking better by the minute.'

It was, Anna thought an hour later, when everyone had moved indoors to shelter from a sudden thunderstorm, rather nice to have someone's undivided attention. Hugo was a bit full of himself, but he was good company, plying her with questions about her life and appearing genuinely interested in her music, her upcoming uni course and her career ambitions.

'Say, that guy over there, the stocky one who keeps looking at you – I swear I've seen him somewhere. Who is he?'

'That's Jamie Benwick,' Anna explained. 'He's been on TV – and he's in the new *ZingaLing* chewing gum ad. He used to go out with Zac's sister.'

'And now?'

'It's a long story,' Anna said, as Jamie caught her eye and made his way towards her. 'And best if you don't mention it.'

'Hi!' Jamie said, 'It's stopped raining and so we're all going down to the Cobb – are you coming?'

'Sure!' Anna agreed and looked questioningly at Hugo. 'You too?'

'Count me in,' he said.

Anna was glad that Hugo was coming. She liked him, even though he didn't seem to be the brightest guy in the world.

Well, Anna thought, *you can't have everything, I guess. Hot body, charm and brains might be too much to ask for.*

There was only one person she knew who managed all three effortlessly.

As they all set off to the harbour – which Anna had explained to Hugo was known as the Cobb – they were walking past the new lifeboat station when Hugo stopped dead in his tracks.

'Damn!'

'What's the matter?' Anna asked.

'Forgot my mobile,' he said. 'I must go and get it – I'm

expecting a call about a job. You go ahead – I'll catch up with you in a bit.'

Hugo had hardly moved three paces away when Jamie launched into a tale of woe about Phoebe.

'I only came because I thought she would be here,' he sighed. 'But Zac says she and Cameron have gone to Umbria. I could never afford to take her somewhere like that. I just can't believe . . .'

'Jamie, listen. You don't want to get boring,' Anna said, as they began climbing the steps up to the outer wall. 'I mean, I know you're upset but life goes on, and you've got a great career and —'

'That's what everyone says,' Jamie replied. 'But you don't understand. It's not just losing Phoebe, it's knowing that if I was a different sort of person she might still be with me.'

Anna said nothing, knowing that he'd explain what he meant in his own good time but rather hoping he wouldn't.

'I'm an only child, no brothers or sisters,' he said. 'And the only thing I've ever been any good at is drama. My mum has always dreamed of me being a star – and when I got the part in *Emmerdale*, she was as excited as if I'd landed *Hamlet* in the West End!'

Anna smiled.

'The thing was, Feebs and I had been planning to go backpacking – just for a month or so – and it clashed with the dates for filming. I wanted to say no to the part but Mum reckoned that, if I refused that chance, I'd mess up any hope of something bigger later on.'

'So you took the part and the backpacking was put on hold?'

'Yeah, and you know what? She wouldn't have gone to stay with her gran if we'd been backpacking, and if she hadn't gone, she would never have met Cameron.'

'It's no good thinking like that,' Anna said wearily. 'We've all made decisions we've come to regret; I guess all you can do is make a promise to yourself never to make the same mistake twice.'

'I guess you're right and I do. Hey, look out!'

He jumped to one side and almost fell over on the wet cobbles as Louisa and Hen hurtled past, giggling loudly, with Leo and Charlie close on their heels.

'Now shut up, you lot,' Louisa ordered when everyone finally caught up with them. 'I'm going to do the Meryl Streep bit.'

'The what?' Henrietta asked.

'You know, in that film Mum drools over,' Louisa said, 'Can't remember what it's called.'

'*The French Lieutenant's Woman*,' Anna murmured.

'Ah, but you don't have the hooded cape or the haunted expression,' Felix laughed.

'See? Felix knew at once what I meant,' Louisa said, slipping her hand into his and ignoring Anna. 'Most guys wouldn't have had a clue. Now who's got a camera? You have to take my picture.'

She walked to the end of the sea wall, her long hair blowing in the wind, and adopted a theatrical pose, the back of her hand held on her brow.

While Louisa played to her audience, especially Felix, Anna drifted away, closed her eyes and switched off. She gulped in the sea air, with her face turned to the sun as the seagulls wheeled and screeched above her head and the waves, larger now as the wind freshened, broke against the side of the Cobb.

'*Aaarghhhh!*' The scream shattered Anna's peaceful thoughts.

'My God, Louisa!' someone shouted.

'Do something, someone do something!'

Anna's eyes shot open and she started running back towards the end of the Cobb even before her brain had processed what was happening. Everyone was peering over the end of the Cobb into the sea – everyone except Louisa.

'She slipped, she's in the water,' Felix gabbled as Anna dashed up.

In a second, Jamie had whipped off his shirt and jumped into the water. Grabbing the seemingly lifeless Louisa under the arms, he pulled her to the side.

'She's unconscious,' he called. 'I need help here.'

Charlie, Zac and Leo bent down and between the three of them they hoisted Louisa up out of the water.

'I should have said something. I was just thinking she was too close to the edge,' Felix muttered, kneeling beside her and gently moving her soaking wet hair off her face.

'I've got my mobile, I'll call an ambulance,' Anna said. 'Oh damn, no signal. Charlie, check her airways – is she breathing? Has she got a pulse?'

'Yes, and yes,' Charlie said, his face paler by the minute.

'Henrietta, take Jamie's shirt and press hard on that head wound, it'll stop the bleeding.'

'I can't, I can't, I feel sick.'

'I'll do it,' Sula said, tears streaming down her face. 'Oh God, why did I ever suggest coming down here?'

'What on earth's happened? What's going on?' Hugo, beads of perspiration on his forehead, came running up to them.

'Louisa fell off the Cobb,' Anna replied. 'Looks like she hit her head on one of those rocks.'

'Can I do something? Here, take this. She needs something under her head.'

He lifted his arms and pulled his rugby shirt over his head. Despite the tension of the moment, Anna couldn't help but notice his finely toned muscles and tanned torso.

'You went back for your mobile, yes?' Anna gasped. 'Have you got a signal?'

'I couldn't get it, could I?' Hugo sighed. 'I forgot the house would be locked up.'

'Don't worry,' Leo said, waving his mobile at her. 'I've got a signal. Ambulance please, and fast. The Cobb. There's a girl half drowned and unconscious.'

What seemed like an eternity – but was in fact only five minutes later – the wailing of a siren alerted them to the fact that people along the Cobb were scattering to left and right to let an ambulance through, and within seconds, two paramedics were at Louisa's side.

'I'm going with her,' Charlie announced, as they lifted Louisa into the vehicle on a stretcher.

'And me,' Mallory said.

'You can't all come,' the senior paramedic pointed out.

'I'm going and Anna should come with me,' Felix announced suddenly, not taking his eyes off Louisa's. 'She'll keep calm. You lot can get a cab and follow on.'

'My car's at the house,' Charlie began.

'Pimm's all afternoon and then a drive – I don't think so,' Anna retorted. 'We can do without another disaster.'

'Told you she had sense,' Felix muttered, to no one in particular.

For a few moments, as the ambulance jolted down the Cobb, Felix and Anna sat in silence, watching and praying as the paramedic put an oxygen mask on Louisa's face.

Suddenly, her eyes opened. 'What's going on?' she said. 'Where am I?'

'Thank God, oh Louisa, Louisa, thank God!' Felix cried and grasped her hand. 'It's OK, it's going to be fine. Everything's going to be fine.'

'Do you sometimes wish . . .? Felix murmured an hour later, as they sat in A&E waiting to hear news of Louisa.

'Wish what?'

'That it was possible to turn the clock back? To wipe out something and do it all over again?'

Anna fixed him with a steady gaze. 'Yes I do. Every day of my life.'

Felix looked back at her. 'You see, the thing is, this afternoon . . .'

He broke off, as Charlie appeared from the cubicle where Louisa had been taken.

'She's going to be fine,' he cried. 'She's got concussion and she'll need stitches to that head wound, but the X-ray's clear – no skull fracture.'

Anna felt her shoulders drop with sheer relief. At the same time her heart, which had momentarily lifted when Felix began speaking, sank to her boots. All he'd been talking about was wiping out the accident.

She was stupid for even hoping that his thoughts had been somewhere else altogether.

The atmosphere back at the house that evening was subdued. Charlie, Henrietta and Felix were still at the hospital with Louisa; Hugo was glued to his mobile, and Zac and Sula were half-heartedly trying to get a barbecue going.

It was as Anna spotted Jamie making his way across the lawn towards her that she realised she had to have some space. She ran into the house, across the hallway and out of the front door.

Ten minutes later, she had kicked off her wedges and was sitting on a broken breakwater on the sandy beach, gazing out to sea, the horizon wavy through the mist of her tears. Whether it was delayed shock from the accident, or whether it was seeing Felix's tenderness towards Louisa in the ambulance, she didn't know; but once she had started to cry, she couldn't stop. Watching the waves lapping the shore, all she could remember were the other times she and Felix had been by the sea – the fish and chips and the kisses at Exmouth, the wonderful moments on the beach before it all went wrong on the Isle of Wight. If she closed her eyes, she could picture every last detail of Felix's face, the smell of him, the way his voice went up at the end of a sentence as if asking a question, the feel of his arms as he wrapped them round her.

'I'm a man on a mission!'

She jumped and turned – Hugo was standing behind her, an ice cream in each hand.

'You were missed and I said I would go and look for you,' he said, passing her a cone. 'Are you OK? Well, no, clearly not – can I help or do you want me to go away?'

She could hardly tell him to go away and, besides, she had promised herself that she would stop wallowing in self-pity. She shook her head. 'I'm all right. And thanks for this.' She licked the ice cream and got to her feet. 'Will you do me a favour?'

'Of course,' Hugo said. 'Whatever you want.'

'Don't tell anyone that I was – you know, in a bit of a state.'

'A state?' Hugo raised an eyebrow. 'I didn't find you in a state. I found you on the beach eating an ice cream.'

As Anna walked with him back to the house, it occurred to her that perhaps she could, if she tried hard enough, get to like Hugo a lot.

When they got inside, they found Sula in tears, and Zac, Mallory and Jamie rushing around like scalded cats.

'What's happened? It's not Louisa, is it?' Anna gasped.

Zac shook his head. 'The house has been burgled,' he said. 'Sula had a wad of money in her bag and it's gone, and my wallet's been emptied.'

'You'd better check your bag,' Leo said, glancing at Anna.

'I've had it with me all day,' Anna said, unzipping it. 'No it's all fine.'

'Thank God for that,' Mallory said. 'I gave you all that cash of mine to look after, and if that had gone I would have . . .'

'I'll go and check my room,' Hugo said, and ran up the stairs two at a time. Within moments, he was back.

'My iPod's gone, and sixty pounds,' he said. 'This is unbelievable. But you know, I've just had a thought. When I came back for my phone . . .'

'The house was locked, surely? I remember doing it,' Sula asked, wiping her eyes. 'If Mum thinks I left it open, she'll kill me.'

'There's no sign of a door being forced,' Zac reasoned, putting his arm round Sula. 'So you must have left the front door on the latch.'

'No, the front door was locked, I mean that's why I couldn't get in to get my phone,' Hugo said. 'But just as I was crossing the road on my way to the house, I saw someone leaving by your side gate. I didn't think anything of it – thought maybe someone had dropped a parcel off or something. But do you think . . .?' He left the words hanging in the air.

'The back door? Oh no, I never checked that.' Sula sighed. 'Did you try it, Hugo?'

Hugo shook his head. 'No,' he said. 'I went straight back to the Cobb and found you lot and Louisa.'

'We ought to check Felix and Charlie's room to see if it looks as if their stuff's been tampered with,' Zac said. 'And Henrietta's, and then phone the police.'

'Hang on,' Hugo said. 'We can hardly go rifling through their belongings and leave fingerprints all over the place. Shouldn't we wait till they get back?'

'I guess,' said Zac.

'Hugo, why don't you phone the police? After all, you were the one who saw this suspicious guy,' Anna suggested. 'We can tell them that we don't know whether anything was taken from the others.'

'Great idea! I'll do it right now.'

Sula nodded. 'And then I'll phone Mum. Better get it over with, I guess.'

The following morning, Charlie, Henrietta and Felix returned to the house from the hospital, exhausted but relieved because Louisa was sitting up and complaining about not being allowed to leave hospital. The police had taken details of the missing stuff over the phone and promised to call by at some point, a point which still hadn't arrived.

Bea Musgrove arrived at the house at seven in the morning, on her way to the hospital, and said that the only way to cope was for Henrietta and Mallory to go back to Uppercross Farm at once to help out with changeover day at the cottages and to work in the tearoom.

'But this is supposed to be my weekend off,' Mallory moaned. 'I work twice as hard as anyone else.'

'Oh do shut up, Mallory!' Henrietta snapped. 'Can't you for once think of anyone but yourself?'

It was agreed that Charlie would stay with his mother and Louisa. Neither Jamie nor Felix showed signs of wanting to leave; so Leo offered to drive Henrietta, Mallory and Anna home, Anna having been too nervous of motorway driving to bring her own car.

'What are you doing?' Anna asked Hugo as everyone was packing up. 'Have you got transport?'

Hugo shook his head. 'I'll catch the train to London and see some mates and then head off to Sussex,' he said.

'Have you got enough money?' she asked. 'I mean, with

yours being stolen – I can lend you some.'

'That's really kind, but luckily I had my credit card with me in my back pocket, so I'm fine.' Hugo paused and smiled at her. 'And I'll see you again next weekend.'

'Next weekend?'

'You said you were going to visit your dad, remember? And I hang out on the boat most weekends so . . .'

'Great,' she smiled. 'That would be really nice.'

'In fact, give me your number and I'll text you as soon as I'm down there,' he said. 'Then we can make a plan.'

'Anna, come on!' Leo was gesturing wildly from the car as Anna scribbled her number on the back of an old envelope. 'We need to get a move on.'

'Coming!' she called, smiling at Hugo. 'See you next weekend then.'

'Can't wait,' Hugo said. 'Seven days and counting.'

It wasn't until Leo stopped for petrol at Ringwood Services that Anna realised why it was she felt strange.

She hadn't thought about Felix for three whole hours.

For the next few days, Anna's feet hardly touched the ground. Apart from dashing to see Shannon for an hour or two, she was tied up helping out at Uppercross Farm. The cottages were all occupied, the tearoom was packed all day and, to make matters worse, Henrietta had a pounding headache and a mild fever.

'Don't worry,' Bea reassured Anna on the telephone. 'The twins have always been like that – one's ill, the other comes out in sympathy. Louisa's doing fine – they're discharging her tomorrow and we'll be home in time for supper.'

'Is Felix . . .?'

Anna had vowed to herself that she wouldn't mention his name but, when it came to it, she had to know what was going on.

'He's been a star,' Bea said. 'Kept Charlie occupied and stopped him fretting – honestly, my kids! They fight like cat and dog and then, when something goes wrong, they're closer than finger to thumb. But he's gone now.'

'Gone?'

'Back to his new base, dear,' Bea said. 'For the parade and medals – did he not tell you?'

'He mentioned it that day in your kitchen, but I didn't know it was this week . . . but he'll be back?'

'I really don't know, sweetheart,' Bea sighed. 'He mentioned that, after the parade, he might go up to Shropshire to see his brother – Oscar, isn't it?'

'Really? I didn't think they were that close.'

'I don't know any details but, according to Charlie, he did say . . .'

'Yes?'

'He said that really there was nothing for him to come back for any more.'

'There it is!' Shannon cried, jabbing a finger at the screen of her laptop a couple of days later. 'No picture of him though.'

'*More than 600 Royal Marines paraded through Plymouth city centre yesterday following their return from a seven-month tour of duty in Afghanistan,*' Anna read. '*The members of 45 Commando reformed after a spell of leave . . .*'

'So that's that then,' said Anna. 'He's gone back and he never even said goodbye.'

'Maybe,' Shannon suggested, 'you should concentrate on this new guy – what's his name? Hugo? After all, you can't brood for ever, and if Felix hears that you're with someone else, who knows . . .?'

'Dream on,' Anna replied. 'But you're right. Felix is history. He always was. It's just that I was too stupid to see it.'

❧ CHAPTER 17 ❧

'You pierce my soul. I am half agony, half hope.'
(Jane Austen, *Persuasion*)

ALTHOUGH ANNA HADN'T WANTED TO GO TO EASTBOURNE, now the time had come she was actually quite relieved to be leaving Kellynch. There was no point in hanging around at Marina's cottage in order to be near to Hampton House in case Felix decided to see her. He wouldn't and she had to move on. Her godmother, back from Madeira and full of a new gardening project to enhance the rockery at Magpie Cottage, made no secret of the fact that she thought it time that Anna left her old life behind her and 'forged ahead' as she put it, into pastures new.

'I'll miss you like crazy,' Shannon said tearfully when Anna went to her house to say goodbye.

'Hey, I'll be back in two weeks,' Anna reminded her. 'We've still got that slot at Youth in the Park, remember? And Mia's party. Not that Marina seems very keen to have me there.'

'So come to mine,' Shannon urged. 'It would be perfect – Mum's birthday's that weekend and Clive's still going on about taking her to Paris. She won't go if I'm home alone, remember.'

'Deal!' Anna said, giving her a hug. 'Tell you what – why don't we organise a final get-together – you know, before we all go off to uni. Or in your case, the Royal College of Music! How grand does that sound?'

'Brilliant!' Shannon said. 'And you can bring your new man to Mia's as well.'

'He's not my man,' Anna protested.

'Yet,' Shannon teased. 'Actually, I've just had the most brilliant idea . . .'

'No, no, no!' Anna held up her hands in mock horror. 'I've had enough of your brilliant ideas to last me for a very long time. Now can we just change the subject?'

'OK,' Shannon said, pulling a face. 'Have you got any chocolate?'

Anna had to admit that the apartment at Sovereign Harbour had a lot going for it. The vast, four-bedroomed penthouse overlooked the busy marina, crammed with yachts and motor cruisers of all descriptions. It was just a couple of minutes stroll from the Yacht Club, and close to all the upmarket boutiques and chandlers, restaurants and wine bars that now, at the end of August, were still packed with holidaymakers and residents. Her father was clearly well pleased with his new situation, eagerly showing off the wet room, the surround sound and the vast plasma TV that took up almost an entire wall in the sitting room. Anna, however, missed the garden and was thankful that the bedroom she was going to share with Mallory had a balcony, complete with marble-topped table and two wicker chairs.

Gabriella was out when Anna arrived, and she had barely finished unpacking when Araminta turned up to whisk Walter off to see *Tristan and Isolde* at Glyndebourne. Anna noted with a sinking heart the fact that her father now called Araminta 'my cherub' and Araminta cloyingly referred to Walter as 'my sweet'.

'And have you told Anna our great secret?' she purred, stroking Walter's arm as he straightened his bow tie in the mirror in the hall. Anna's heart missed a beat.

'Shh now, my cherub, not yet,' Walter urged her. 'We must save it until Mallory arrives. When is she coming?'

'Thursday evening,' Anna said. 'And the Musgroves are all coming to the party and taking her back with them.'

'Splendid, splendid,' he said, rubbing his hands together. 'Oh, and just one thing.' He paused, his forehead puckering in a slight frown. 'Mallory will be with Charlie, of course, and Gabriella has a delightful new friend – William Buxton. His father is Buxton's Cider, you know. Anyway, if you'd like to bring anyone . . .'

'Actually, I might,' Anna smiled. 'I met someone who lives near here – his parents have a boat . . .'

She hated herself for mentioning it, but knew that her father would be impressed. Life was much easier when her father approved of what she did.

Not, of course, that she would go through life being obedient; but maybe hanging out with Hugo would serve a double purpose. She could win back her dad's approval and, at the same time, put Felix well and truly out of her mind.

And it seemed to work. Far from waiting until the

weekend, it was early on Thursday that she received a text from Hugo.

Will b at S Harbour 1p.m. Meet u outside Seamoors wine bar?

'It's so good to see you,' he said, giving her a hug. 'I haven't been able to get you out of my mind ever since you left Lyme Regis. Drink?'

'White wine and soda please,' she replied.

'And how's Louisa?'

'She's doing OK,' Anna assured him. 'The stitches are out but she still looks bruised from her forehead to her cheek. It could have been a lot worse.'

'And the police? Did they sort out the robbery?'

Anna shrugged. 'They went to the house apparently, took details but didn't hold out any hope of finding the cash. Do you know, they didn't even get there till the Sunday evening?'

'I guess that they had bigger fish to fry,' he said, leading her to a table. 'Annoyed about my iPod though.' He took a swig of beer. 'So,' he said. 'Lunch here and then what? Movie? Shopping? Whatever you want – I just want to spend time with you and get to know you better.'

For a moment, Felix's voice, saying much the same thing all those months before, echoed in her head. *Stop it*, she ordered herself. *Don't think about him.*

'Let's go up to Beachy Head,' she suggested hurriedly. 'It's such a lovely day.'

'And tomorrow,' he said, passing her the menu and beckoning to a waitress, 'I'll take you out in the boat. If you're up for it, that is?'

'Oh sure,' she said. 'I'm up for anything. Anything at all.'

<u>To: saxygirl@tiscali.net</u>
<u>From: shannonsmith@email.com</u>
Hi! How's it going? How's Hugo? Is it full on yet? Mia says bring him to the party. Oh, and by the way, you know the guy I told you about? Toby? Turns out Mia's brother's best friend knows him and he's going to fix it that he comes to the party. So watch this space! Miss you. Write or else . . .!
Shannon xx

<u>To: shannonsmith@email.com</u>
<u>From: saxygirl@tiscali.net</u>
Hugo's really nice. Almost too nice. I'm not sure why I feel that but he's almost too attentive, too charming . . . and when we bumped into Dad and Araminta on the Waterfront he was positively gushy. And he talks a lot, but he doesn't actually DO much. Anyway, it's probably me being stupid. I guess I just keep comparing him to Felix . . .

<u>To: saxygirl@tiscali.net</u>
<u>From: shannonsmith@email.com</u>
Anna Eliot, what are you like? You get someone who's all over you and all you think about is comparing him with someone who dumped you? Hello?

<u>To: shannonsmith@email.com</u>
<u>From: saxygirl@tiscali.net</u>
Yes, OK. I know, I'm crazy. Anyway, he's coming to Dad's party. Turns out it's not a housewarming, that was just a red herring. It's a publicity thing – because he's got a job! Presenting a programme for Coast TV twice a week; and what's more he's writing a book! It's going to be his

autobiography – well, to be honest, a ghost writer will be doing the hard part. All Dad will have to do is talk his head off about his life. No problem there then! He seems really happy and we're all over the moon because we thought his 'little secret' was going to be that he and Araminta were getting married and that would have been awful. Sorry – phone ringing, must dash.

Loads of love, xxx

'I'm so so sorry,' Hugo said apologetically the moment Anna answered the phone. 'Sailing's off, I'm afraid. My dad only came down yesterday and took the yacht over to France – birthday surprise for my mum. Not a word to me, of course, till I get a text this morning!'

'Don't worry,' Anna assured him. 'Another time. We could always hire bikes and go —'

'Sorry, I can't,' Hugo interrupted hurriedly. 'Dad's asked me to do all sorts of last minute stuff for him – but I'll see you at the party tomorrow, right? Seven at the Yacht Club?'

'Sure,' Anna said. 'See you then.'

As she snapped her phone shut, she couldn't help wondering just why she didn't feel even the slightest bit disappointed about the last minute change of plan.

'I am so relieved that Dad and Araminta aren't getting married,' Mallory said, as she, Anna and Gaby were getting ready for the party.

'Well, not yet at least,' Gaby commented. 'Dad wants to but you know what?'

Anna and Mallory gasped in horror.

'Araminta wants a pre-nup to ensure Dad can't get his hands on her money. Like how selfish is that?'

'Hey,' said Anna. 'I hadn't credited the woman with that much common sense. Can I borrow your eye-liner?'

'Well, isn't this wonderful!' Marina, who had arrived in Eastbourne a couple of hours before the party and ensconced herself in the Hydro Hotel, surveyed the guests at the Yacht Club with satisfaction. 'Quite like the old days.'

'I'm worried though,' Anna confessed. 'I mean, can Dad afford all this?'

'Oh darling, didn't he tell you?' Marina asked. 'The publishers and the TV company between them are footing the bill. Your father's been offered quite a hefty advance for the book, you know – six figures!'

Anna stared at her in disbelief. 'You're kidding, right!'

'I make it a point never to joke where money is concerned,' Marina laughed. 'He's over the moon – not just about the money, but you know how being the centre of attention suits him?'

She patted her newly coiffeured hair and smiled at Anna. 'Now then, are you going to introduce me to this new boyfriend of yours? Where is he?'

'Over there, talking to Charlie Musgrove,' she said.

'The tall guy? Oh, Anna, he's gorgeous, isn't he?'

'Marina!'

'What? I'm just saying – he looks very much your sort of guy. And I'm thrilled for you.'

'Anna, I have to tell you. If I don't tell someone, I am going to burst!'

Louisa Musgrove pushed Anna into the Ladies and shut the door. 'I'm in love!'

Anna felt sick. She forced a smile on to her lips and tried to look happy.

'I can't believe it,' Louisa gabbled. 'I mean, I've thought in the past that I was keen on him – but this . . . I mean, it's completely different. I just love him so much. I don't care what Mum and Dad say, he's right for me. I just know he is.'

'When did you realise – I mean, when did you fall in love?'

'When I was in hospital,' Louisa said. 'Well, actually, I was beginning to fancy him that day on the Cobb. And then, after the accident, he was so sweet, so attentive.'

'He is really kind . . .' Anna almost choked on the words.

'And then, when I got home, he came to see me every day and . . .'

'He came to see you? What, all that way?' Now she felt bitterly jealous.

'Oh come off it,' Louisa laughed. 'Drayton Magna to Kellynch is all of two miles.'

'Drayton? So who exactly are you in love with?'

'Didn't I say? Jamie, of course. Jamie Benwick. I miss him so much – and we've only been apart for eight hours!'

The surge of joy that coursed through Anna's veins made her feel almost giddy.

'Oh Louisa, that's wonderful! I'm so so happy for you.'
And even more happy for me, she thought.

'But – I thought – I mean, is he really the one for you?'

'Definitely,' Louisa said. 'I don't want anyone else.'

'That's the most wonderful news I've heard in weeks,' Anna said.

* * *

'If I don't get some fresh air, I'll pass out,' Anna murmured to Hugo an hour later. 'And there's only so much polite small talk a girl can stand. Shall we go outside?'

Hugo winked at her and took her hand. Outside on the quayside, she felt a cool breeze against her skin.

'This is better,' she sighed, closing her eyes and turning her face up to the sky and breathing in the sea air.

'This is much better,' Hugo repeated. In an instant he had spun her round to face him and was kissing her hungrily on the lips. It took Anna by surprise, but for a moment she responded, telling herself that maybe this was the way to get Felix out of her head and her heart once and for all, since single or not, he clearly had not time for her.

'I've been wanting to do this for so long,' he murmured, his hands fumbling with the buttons on her shirt as he pushed her into the shadows against the wall. And in the same moment, Anna realised that this was not what she wanted. She tried to pull away, but he was gripping her to him tightly.

'Hugo, no!' she gasped.

'Come off it,' he muttered. 'You know you want . . .'

As his hands moved lower, she stamped on his foot with her heel and turned and ran. She wasn't frightened, she was incandescent – furious with herself for getting into that position and furious with Hugo for assuming that she was that easy.

All at once, she wanted to be alone. Ignoring Hugo's shouts, she ran across the bridge that spanned the harbour and headed for the apartment.

'Miss?' The night porter sounded anxious. 'Are you all right, miss?'

'Fine,' she replied, punching the lift button.

As she pushed open her front door, she saw a letter lying on the doormat. The writing on the envelope was unmistakeable – it was from Felix.

She was ripping it open when her mobile beeped with a text message. That too was from Felix.

Forget what I said in the letter. You've obviously found someone else.

Heart racing, she started to read.

Hi. I can't stand this any longer. I'm due back at my unit in ten days when my physio's finished and who knows where they'll send me? I love you, Anna.

Anna gasped out loud – and then glanced back at the message on the mobile still in her hand.

I never stopped loving you, the letter went on. *Even when I was angry about all that stuff with your dad and you, I never stopped loving you. I tried to – I even tried to fancy Louisa, but nice as she is, it was always you that I thought about. And then that day when you turned up at Charlie's place and fell flat on your face, that's when I knew I still wanted you. Please, say we can try again? Please?*

Anna's mind was racing. This was wonderful except that from his text he thought she'd found someone else and —

'Oh my God!' She spoke the words out loud as the full force of what had happened hit her. There was no stamp on the letter. It had been hand delivered. Which meant Felix had been here. Could he have seen her and Hugo? Outside? Just now?

She ran down the stairs, too panicky to wait for the lift. Once outside she looked frantically up and down the walkway, but there was no sign of him. Not that she really expected there would be. She grabbed her mobile.

You've got it all wrong. I love you u only u. Where r u?

She dashed back into the block of flats.

'Did you see a tall guy, delivering a letter to our flat?' she gabbled at the night porter.

'Oh, you got it, good,' he said.

'Please, did he say where he was going?' Even as she asked the question, she knew it was unlikely.

The porter shook his head.

'OK, thanks,' Anna replied miserably.

'But he did mutter about needing a drink and I gave him a discount voucher for that new place, Slinky Sam.

'Thanks!' Anna belted down the steps and ran full pelt towards the bar.

She found him sitting staring disconsolately into a pint.

'Felix!'

He started, and stared at her. 'I don't want to hear it,' he said, standing up and trying to push past her.

'Felix, listen,' she urged. 'You don't get it.'

'Oh I get it,' he said. 'I saw it with my own eyes. You – and that jerk, Hugo. Kissing.'

'Please, you have to believe me, I didn't want him to,' she said. 'He —'

'Come off it,' Felix said. 'Are you trying to tell me you gave him no encouragement at all? What do you think I am? Dumb?'

'OK, OK, please just let me say this, and then – well, then it's up to you.'

He said nothing, but he didn't move.

'OK, for just a moment, I thought that if I – you know, kissed him, it might help me to forget you. Because I thought you didn't want me and that going out with someone else would help me move on. But it didn't work, because there's only one person I want to kiss, and that's you.'

'Say that again.'

'The only person I want to kiss is you.'

Slowly, very slowly, Felix stretched out a hand and touched her cheek. Electric shocks rippled through Anna's body. Slowly, he wrapped his arms round her and pulled her against him, burying his face in her hair and rocking her gently to and fro.

'You and me? Can we start over?' Felix asked gently. 'I'll keep a low profile.'

'No!'

'What? I thought you said you loved me?'

'I mean, yes please, we can start over, but no you won't keep a low profile.' Anna grabbed his hand. 'Come on.'

'Come on where?'

'We're going back to the party. I want the whole world to see how much you mean to me.'

'Anna, that's asking for trouble . . .'

She shook her head. 'No. Doing what I was told all those months was asking for trouble. You are the most important person in my life and it's time everyone knew it.'

Walter was deep in conversation with Araminta, Marina and someone from *Coast TV* as Anna and Felix edged their way through the guests.

'Dad,' Anna said, gripping Felix's hand. 'You remember Felix Wentworth?'

'Congratulations, sir – on the programme and the book,' Felix said. holding his gaze. 'You must be delighted.'

For a moment, Walter simply stared at him. Then, slowly, he nodded and then he smiled. 'Thank you, Felix, I am – it's a new start for me. It's time to move on from my past mistakes. You're a brave, loyal young man. I think we all need new starts from time to time, don't you?'

He offered Felix his hand and Anna thought she might burst with joy.

'Well, Anna, what are you waiting for?' her father asked. 'Get the poor man a drink. He looks as though he could do with one.'

'One down, one to go,' Anna said softly a few minutes later as she and Felix stood on the balcony of the Yacht Club. 'There's still someone who's not going to be happy. You know – that we're together again.'

'What do you mean?' Felix asked, his fingers gently caressing her hair. 'My mother will be very pleased. She knows she manipulated you, and she felt responsible for us splitting up. I did blame her for quite a while, too. We're getting on fine now, though.'

'No, I meant Ruth,' Anna said. 'I'm pretty sure she thinks I'm no good for you.'

'That's where you're wrong,' Felix laughed. 'She was the one who urged me to come down here. She knew about the party from the Musgroves and she said she was fed up with me moping about. She said if I didn't get in the car and head down here, she'd drag me here herself!'

'I can't believe it!' Anna sighed. 'I'm so happy.' She was silent as she hugged Felix to her.

'Say, I wonder where Hugo got to?' she said after a while. 'I guess to be fair I ought to . . .'

'Excuse me,' Felix said, 'but if you just take a look down there.' He pointed to the waterfront. Hugo was in animated conversation with one of the girls from *Coast TV*, and he didn't look like someone suffering from the pains of rejection.

'Now if you don't mind, could we just concentrate on us?' Felix said. 'After all, we have got an awful lot of catching up to do.'

And with that, he pulled her towards him and kissed her gently. And Anna knew that this was all she would ever want as long as she lived.

❧ CHAPTER 18 ❧

'It was overpowering happiness . . .'
(Jane Austen, *Persuasion*)

'SO COME ON,' MIA SAID A COUPLE OF WEEKS LATER, AFTER
Anna had hugged her and handed over her birthday
present. 'Where is he? Let's see this new man.'

'Don't tell me he's not here,' Lauren added.

'Maybe that's no bad thing,' Shannon ventured
nervously. 'Maybe Anna's decided to come on her own.'

Anna laughed. 'He's just parking the car.'

'Before he comes, can I have a quick word?' Shannon
looked unusually anxious as she dragged Anna to one side.
'About Hugo, I mean I know you're keen and everything
but . . .'

'But what?' Anna asked, smiling to herself.

'OK, you're not going to like this,' Shannon said. 'But
I'm your friend and friends tell it like it is. You know the
guy I told you about? Toby?'

Anna nodded.

'We're together,' Shannon grinned. 'He's over there –
I'll introduce you in a minute.'

'That's wonderful!' Anna hugged her, glancing across at

a sandy-haired boy who was adjusting the speakers on the music system. 'I'm so pleased – but what's that got to do with Hugo?'

'Toby knows Hugo,' she said. 'Anna, he's got history.'

'Haven't we all?' Anna shrugged.

'Look, last week Toby was at a cricket club party, and Hugo was there, getting very drunk.'

'Guys do sometimes,' Anna remarked, stringing her along. 'That doesn't make them bad people!'

'Yeah, well, he happened to be drunk enough to regale everyone at the bar with the story of how he nicked money off a bunch of mates at a house party in Lyme Regis and –

This time, Anna's reaction was totally genuine. She stared at Shannon in horror. 'Oh my God. I don't believe it.'

'So, I had to tell you,' Shannon said. 'You do understand? It's because I care about you. I'd hate to see you hooked up with someone who didn't deserve you.'

'That's OK then,' Anna laughed, peering out of the front door and beckoning wildly. Grabbing Felix by the hand, she dragged him into the hall.

'You remember Felix, don't you?' she asked her friends with a wicked grin. 'My boyfriend?'

'You're back together?' Lauren gasped.

'Anna, you shady lady! Why didn't you tell me? This is so so cool,' Shannon said, laughing.

'I thought – I mean . . . oh this is so romantic,' Mia sighed.

Felix grinned and put his arm round Anna, pulling her towards him.

'And you won't believe what Shannon's just told me about Hugo!' Anna said.

'That he's a complete sham, a fake and a total waste of space, perhaps?' Felix asked dryly.

'How did you know?' Shannon and Anna asked simultaneously.

'When the girl I love suddenly hooks up with a guy that I'm deeply suspicious about, I make it my business to discover what's going on.'

'That,' said Mia, 'is so totally romantic.'

'Mia, if you say that one more time, I'll slap you,' Lauren muttered.

'But what made you suspicious? I mean, you hardly know him,' Anna reasoned.

'That afternoon at Sula's house, before we went down to the garden, Hugo barged into my room, right?' Felix explained. 'I didn't think anything of it – he said he'd got in a muddle. But then Jamie happened to let slip that he'd found him in his room, and then Louisa said he nearly caught her in her . . . Well, anyway, I got to thinking. I mean – there were only five bedrooms, for God's sake. How many mistakes can you make?'

'You think he was checking out what was what?' Anna asked.

Felix sighed. 'Yes, except that I didn't work that out till I was halfway home,' he admitted. 'I was so taken up with Louisa and feeling guilty about the accident.'

'Guilty?' Shannon asked. 'How come?'

'Felix thinks if he hadn't gone on about how Meryl Streep looked on the posters of *The French Lieutenant's Woman*, she wouldn't have started showing off, and wouldn't have fallen in,' Anna sighed.

'Rubbish,' Shannon said in her down to earth way.

'Anyway, is that why you went to Eastbourne? To confront the Horrible Hugo?'

'No,' Felix said. 'I went to Eastbourne to find Anna and beg for another chance! And you know what? It took all my charms but I finally persuaded her.'

'*You* persuaded *me*?' Anna teased back, and then looked serious for a moment. 'No one is ever going to persuade me to do anything ever again – not unless it's something I want.'

She squeezed Felix's hand and looked up at him lovingly.

'And you, Felix Wentworth, are what I really, really want.'

❧ ACKNOWLEDGEMENTS ❧

This book would never have been finished had it not been for the help, encouragement and knowledge of a whole bunch of wonderful people.

My thanks go to John Leach (YO, May '96) for his unending patience and detailed information about life in the Royal Marines; to Dr Chris Winfield for his insights into life in a war zone; to Caroline Davis and Pippa Kirby for being so passionate about *Persuasion*; to Sally Bird for tea and gluten free cake when things got tough; to Lorraine Bewley and Year 9 at Northampton School for Girls for inventing Wild Chicks and to a whole host of members of the Scattered Authors' Society for their humour, encouragement and common sense.

As usual, I am hugely indebted to Ruth Williams and Brenda Gardner of Piccadilly Press for curtailing my inappropriate flights of fancy, and to my long suffering agent, Jane Judd, who copes with my neuroses on an ongoing basis.

☆

www.piccadillypress.co.uk

☆ The latest news on forthcoming books

☆ Chapter previews

☆ Author biographies

☆ Fun quizzes

☆ Reader reviews

☆ Competitions and fab prizes

☆ Book features and cool downloads

☆ And much, much more . . .

Log on and check it out!

Piccadilly Press

☆